ELSEWHERE

ELSEWHERE

GABRIELLE ZEVIN

BLOOMSBURY

First published in Great Britain in 2005 by Bloomsbury Publishing Plc
36 Soho Square, London, W1D 3QY

First published in America in 2005 by Farrar, Straus and Giroux, LLC

A CIP catalogue record of this book is available from the British Library

Hardback ISBN 0 7475 7700 5
ISBN 9780747577003

Export paperback ISBN
0 7475 8034 0
9780747580348

Printed in Great Britain by Clays Ltd, St Ives plc

10 9 8 7 6 5 4 3 2 1

All papers used by Bloomsbury Publishing are natural, recyclable products made from
wood grown in well-managed forests. The manufacturing processes conform to the
environmental regulations of the country of origin.

www.bloomsbury.com/elsewhere

To HCC

Contents

Prologue: In the End

'The end came quickly, and there wasn't any pain.' Sometimes, the father whispers it to the mother. Sometimes, the mother to the father. From the top of the stairs, Lucy hears it all and says nothing.

For Lizzie's sake, Lucy wants to believe that the end was quick and painless: a quick end is a good end. But she can't help wondering, How do they know? The moment of the crash certainly must have been painful, Lucy reasons. And what if that one moment hadn't been quick at all?

She wanders into Lizzie's room and surveys it despondently. A teenage girl's whole life is a collection of odds and ends: a turquoise bra thrown over a computer monitor, an unmade bed, an aquarium filled with earthworms, a deflated Mylar balloon from last Valentine's Day, a Do Not Enter sign on the doorknob, a pair of unused tickets for a Machine concert under the bed. In the end, what does it all mean anyway? And what does it matter? Is a person just a pile of junk?

The only thing to do when Lucy feels this way is to dig. Dig until she forgets everything and everyone. Dig right through the pink carpet. Dig until she reaches the ceiling of the floor below. Dig until she falls through. Dig and dig and dig and dig.

Lucy has finally worked up a good cleansing dig when Alvy (the seven-year-old brother) picks her up off the rug and sets her in his lap. 'Don't worry,' Alvy says. 'Even though you belonged to Lizzie, someone will always feed you and wash you and take you to the park. You can even sleep in *my* room now.'

Sitting primly on Alvy's too-small lap, Lucy imagines that Lizzie is just away at college. Lizzie was nearly sixteen, and it would have happened in about two years anyway. The glossy brochures had already begun piling up on Lizzie's bedroom floor. Occasionally, Lucy would urinate on one of the brochures or bite a corner out of another, but even then she knew it couldn't be stopped. One day Lizzie would go, and dogs weren't allowed in dorm rooms.

'Where do you think she is?' Alvy asks.

Lucy cocks her head.

'Is she'—he pauses—'up there?'

As far as Lucy knows, the only thing up there is the attic.

'Well,' Alvy says, jutting his chin defiantly toward the sky, 'I believe she *is* up there. And I believe there are angels there and harps and heaps of puffy clouds and white silky pajamas and everything.'

Likely story, Lucy thinks. She doesn't believe in the happy hunting ground or the rainbow bridge. She believes a pug goes around once and that's it. She wishes she might see Lizzie again someday, but she doesn't hold out much hope. Even if there is something after the end, who knows if it has kibble or naps or fresh water or cushy laps or even dogs? And the worst part of all, it isn't *here*!

Lucy moans, mainly in grief but partially (it must be said) in hunger. When a family loses its only daughter, a pug's mealtimes can be erratic. Lucy curses her treacherous stomach: what kind of beast is she to be hungry when her best friend is dead?

'I wish you could talk,' Alvy says. 'I bet you're thinking something interesting.'

'And I wish you could listen,' Lucy barks, but Alvy doesn't understand her anyway.

The next day the mother takes Lucy to the dog park. It's the first time anyone has remembered to walk Lucy since the end.

On the way over, Lucy can smell the mother's sadness all around them. She tries to determine what the smell reminds her of. Is it rain? Parsley? Bourbon? Old books? Wool socks? Bananas, Lucy decides.

At the park, Lucy just lies on a bench, feeling friendless and depressed and (will it never end?) a little hungry. A toy poodle named Coco asks Lucy what's wrong, and with a sigh Lucy tells her. As the poodle is a notorious gossip, the news spreads quickly through the dog park.

Bandit, a one-eyed all-American who in less refined circles would be called a mutt, offers his sympathies. He asks Lucy, 'They putting you on the streets?'

'No,' Lucy replies, 'I'll still live with the same family.'

'Then I don't see what's so bad about it,' Bandit says.

'She was only fifteen.'

'So? *We* only have ten, fifteen years tops, and you don't see us carrying on.'

'But she wasn't a dog,' Lucy barks. 'She was a human, my human, and she got hit by a car.'

'So? *We* get hit by cars all the time. Cheer up, little pug. You worry too much. That's why you have so many wrinkles.'

Lucy has heard this joke many times before and she thinks, somewhat unkindly, for Bandit isn't a bad sort, that she has never met a mutt with a good sense of humor.

'My advice is to find yourself another two-legger. If you'd lived my life, you'd know they're all about the same anyway. When the kibble runs out, I'm gone.' With that, Bandit abandons Lucy to join a game of Frisbee.

Lucy sighs and feels very sorry for herself. She watches the other dogs playing in the dog park. 'Look how they can sniff each other's rear ends and chase balls and run around in circles! How innocent they seem!

'In the natural order of things, a dog isn't meant to outlive her human!' Lucy howls. 'No one understands unless it's happened to her. And what's more, no one even seems to care.' Lucy shakes her small round head. 'It's so totally disheartening. I can't even be bothered to curl my tail.

'In the end, the end of a life only matters to friends, family, and other folks you used to know,' the pug whimpers miserably. 'For everyone else, it's just another end.'

Part I: The *Nile*

At Sea

Elizabeth Hall wakes in a strange bed in a strange room with the strange feeling that her sheets are trying to smother her.

Liz (who is Elizabeth to her teachers; Lizzie at home, except when she's in trouble; and just plain Liz everywhere else in the world) sits up in bed, bumping her head on an unforeseen upper bunk. From above, a voice she does not recognize protests, 'Aw hell!'

Liz peers into the top bunk, where a girl she has never seen before is sleeping, or at least trying to. The sleeping girl, who is near Liz's own age, wears a white nightgown and has long dark hair arranged in a thatch of intricately beaded braids. To Liz, she looks like a queen.

'Excuse me,' Liz asks, 'but would you happen to know where we are?'

The girl yawns and rubs the sleep out of her eyes. She glances from Liz to the ceiling to the floor to the window and then to Liz again. She touches her braids and sighs. 'On a boat,' she answers, stifling another yawn.

'What do you mean 'on a boat'?'

'There's water, lots and lots of it. Just look out the window,' she replies before cocooning herself in the bedclothes. 'Of course, you might have thought to do that without waking me.'

'Sorry,' Liz whispers.

Liz looks out the porthole that is parallel to her bed. Sure enough, she sees hundreds of miles of early-morning darkness and ocean in all directions, blanketed by a healthy coating of fog. If she squints, Liz can make out a boardwalk. There, she sees the forms of her parents and her little brother, Alvy. Ghostly and becoming smaller by the second, her father is crying and her mother is holding him. Despite the apparent distance, Alvy seems to be looking at Liz and waving. Ten seconds later, the fog swallows her family entirely.

Liz lies back in bed. Even though she feels remarkably awake, she knows she is dreaming, for several reasons: one, there is no earthly way she would be on a boat when she is supposed to be finishing tenth grade; two, if this is a vacation, her parents and Alvy, unfortunately, should be with her; and three, only in dreams can you see things you shouldn't see, like your family on a boardwalk from hundreds of miles away. Just as Liz reaches four, she decides to get out of bed. What a waste, she thinks, to spend one's dreams asleep.

Not wanting to further disturb the sleeping girl, Liz tiptoes across the room toward the bureau. The telltale sign that she is, indeed, at sea comes from the furniture: it is bolted to the floor. While she does not find the room unpleasant, Liz thinks it feels lonely and sad, as if many people had passed through it but none had decided to stay.

Liz opens the bureau drawers to see if they are empty. They are: not even a Bible. Although she tries to be very quiet, she loses her grip on the last drawer and it slams shut. This has the unfortunate effect of waking the sleeping girl again.

'People are sleeping here!' the girl yells.

'I'm sorry. I was just checking the drawers. In case you were wondering, they're empty,' Liz apologizes, and sits on the lower bunk. 'I like your hair by the way.'

The girl fingers her braids. 'Thanks.'

'What's your name?' Liz asks.

'Thandiwe Washington, but I'm called Thandi.'

'I'm Liz.'

Thandi yawns. 'You sixteen?'

'In August,' Liz replies.

'I turned sixteen in January.' Thandi looks into Liz's bunk. 'Liz,' she says, turning the one syllable of Liz's name into a slightly southern two, *Li-iz*, 'you mind if I ask you a personal question?'

'Not really.'

'The thing is'—Thandi pauses—'well, are you a skinhead or something?'

'A skinhead? No, of course not.' Liz raises a single eyebrow. 'Why would you ask that?'

'Like, 'cause you don't have hair.' Thandi points to Liz's head which is completely bald except for the earliest sprouts of light blond growth.

Liz strokes her head with her hand, enjoying the odd smoothness of it. What hair there is feels like the feathers on a newborn chick. She gets out of bed and looks at her reflection in the mirror. Liz sees a slender girl of about sixteen with very pale skin and greenish blue eyes. The girl, indeed, has no hair.

'That's strange,' Liz says. In real life, Liz has long, straight blond hair that tangles easily.

'Didn't you know?' Thandi asks.

Liz considers Thandi's question. In the very back of her mind, she recalls lying on a cot in the middle of a blindingly bright room as her father shaved her head. No. Liz remembers that it wasn't her father. She thought it was her father, because it had been a man near her father's age. Liz definitely remembers crying, and hearing her mother say, 'Don't worry, Lizzie, it will all grow back.' No, that isn't right either. Liz hadn't cried; her mother had been the one crying. For a moment, Liz tries to remember if this episode actually happened. She decides she doesn't want to think about it any longer, so she asks Thandi, 'Do you want to see what else is on the boat?'

'Why not? I'm up now.' Thandi climbs down from her bunk.

'I wonder if there's a hat in here somewhere,' says Liz. Even in a dream, Liz isn't sure she wants to be the freaky bald girl. She opens the closet and looks under the bed: both are as empty as the bureau.

'Don't feel bad about your hair, Liz,' Thandi says gently.

'I don't. I just think it's weird,' Liz says.

'Hey, I've got weird things, too.' Thandi raises her canopy of braids like a theater curtain. 'Ta da,' she says, revealing a small but deep, still-red wound at the base of her skull.

Although the wound is less than a half inch in diameter, Liz can tell it must have been the result of an extremely serious injury.

'God, Thandi, I hope that doesn't hurt.'

'It did at first; it hurt like hell, but not anymore.' Thandi lowers her hair. 'I think it's getting better actually.'

'How did you get that?'

'Don't remember,' says Thandi, rubbing the top of her head as if she could stimulate her memory with her hands. 'It might have happened a long time ago, but it could have been yesterday, too, know what I mean?'

Liz nods. Although she doesn't think Thandi makes any sense, Liz sees no point in arguing with the crazy sorts of people one meets in a dream.

'We should go,' Liz says.

On the way out, Thandi casts a cursory glance at herself in the mirror. 'You think it matters that we're both wearing pjs?' she asks.

Liz looks at Thandi's white nightgown. Liz herself is wearing white men's-style pajamas. 'Why would it matter?' Liz asks, thinking it far worse to be bald than underdressed. 'Besides, Thandi, what else do you wear while you're dreaming?' Liz places her hand on the doorknob. Someone somewhere once told Liz that she must never, under any circumstances, open a door in a dream. Since Liz can't remember who the person was or why all doors must remain closed, she decides to ignore the advice.

Curtis Jest

Liz and Thandi find themselves in a hallway with hundreds of doors exactly like the one they just closed.

'How do you think we'll find it again?' Thandi asks.

'I doubt I'll have to,' Liz answers. 'I'll probably wake up before that, don't you think?'

'Well, just in case you don't, our room number's 130002,' Thandi says.

Liz points to a hand-painted sign at the end of the hallway.

ATTENTION
ALL PASSAGERS OF THE SS *NILE*!
THE DINING ROOM IS UP THREE FLIGHTS
ON THE LIDO DECK

'Hungry?' Thandi asks.

'Starved.' Liz is surprised by her own response. She cannot recall being hungry in a dream before.

The most remarkable thing about the ship's dining room is the people: they are all old. A few are her parents' age, but most are even older than them. Gray hair or no hair, brown spots, and sagging skin are the norm. It is by far the largest number of old people Liz has ever seen gathered in one place, even counting visits to her grandmother in Boca. Liz scans the dining room. 'Are we in the wrong place?' she asks.

Thandi shrugs. 'Beats me, but they're coming this way.' Sure enough, three women are making a beeline for Thandi and Liz. They remind Liz of the witches in *Macbeth*, a play she just finished reading for tenth-grade honors English.

'Hello, darlings,' says a pygmy-like woman with a New York accent, 'I'm Doris, and this is Myrna, and this is Florence.' Standing on her tiptoes, Doris reaches up to pat Liz's molted head. 'Good Lord, would you look how young she is?'

Liz smiles politely but takes a step back so as to discourage further patting.

'How old are you?' Doris the pygmy squints up at Liz. 'Twelve?'

'I'm fifteen,' Liz corrects her. 'Almost sixteen. I look older with hair.'

The one called Florence pipes up, 'What happened to you girls?' She has the scratchy voice of a lifelong smoker.

'What do you mean "happened"?' Liz demands.

'I was shot in the head, ma'am,' Thandi volunteers.

'Speak up,' says Myrna who has a fuzzy white caterpillar of a mustache. 'My hearing's not so good.'

'I WAS SHOT IN THE HEAD.'

Liz turns to Thandi. 'I thought you said you didn't remember how you got the hole in your head.'

Thandi apologizes, 'I *just* remembered.'

'Shot in the head!' Florence-scratchy-voice says. 'Oy, that's rough.'

'Aw, it's nothing special. Happens pretty regularly where I'm from,' Thandi says.

'WHAT?' asks Myrna with the mustache. 'Say it toward my left ear, that's the good one.'

'I SAID, "IT'S NOTHING SPECIAL," ' Thandi yells.

'Maybe you should go to the healing center?' Florence suggests. 'There's one on the Portofino deck. Myrna's already been twice.'

Thandi shakes her head. 'I think it's healing just fine on its own.'

Liz doesn't understand this conversation at all. Her stomach growls loudly. 'Excuse me,' she says.

Doris the pygmy waves her hand toward the buffet line. 'You girls go get something to eat. Remember, you gotta get here early for the good stuff.'

For breakfast, Liz selects pancakes and tapioca pudding. Thandi has sushi, truffles, and baked beans. Liz eyes Thandi's food selections curiously. 'That's certainly an interesting combination,' Liz says.

'At home, we never get half the things they have on that buffet,' says Thandi, 'and I'm planning to try all of it before we get there.'

14

'Thandi,' Liz asks casually, 'where do you think "there" is?'

Thandi considers Liz's question for a moment. 'We're on a boat,' Thandi says, 'and boats have to be going somewhere.'

The girls secure a table near a bay window, slightly away from the other diners. Liz polishes off her pancakes in record time. She feels as if she hasn't eaten in weeks.

Scraping the bottom of her pudding cup, Liz looks at Thandi. 'So, I've never known anyone who was shot in the head before.'

'Can we talk about it after I'm done eating?' Thandi asks.

'Sorry,' Liz says, 'just making conversation.'

Liz stares out the window. The fog has lifted, and the water is clearer than any water she has ever seen. It is strange, Liz thinks, how much the sky looks like the sea. A sea, she thinks, is rather like a soggy sky, and a sky rather like a wrung-out sea. Liz wonders where the ship is going and if she will wake up before it arrives and what her mother will say this dream probably means. Her mother is a child psychologist and knows about these things. Liz's reverie is interrupted by a man's voice.

'You mind?' he asks with an English accent. 'You ladies seem to be the only people under eighty in this place.'

'Of course not. We're all done here any . . .' Liz's voice trails off as she sees the man for the first time. He is around thirty years old with sparkling blue eyes that match his spiky blue hair. Liz, like most people her age, would recognize those eyes anywhere. 'You're Curtis Jest, aren't you?'

The man with the blue hair smiles. 'Used to be, I suppose.' Curtis holds out his hand. 'And who might you be?'

'I'm Liz, and this is Thandi, and I honestly can't believe I'm meeting you. Machine's about my favorite band in the whole world!' Liz gushes.

Curtis sprinkles salt on his french fries and smiles. 'My, that is a compliment,' he says, 'for the world is a very large place. I always preferred the Clash myself, Liz.'

'This is the coolest dream ever,' says Liz, feeling pleased that her subconscious has introduced Curtis Jest to the dream.

Curtis cocks his head. 'Dream, you say?'

Thandi whispers to Curtis, 'She doesn't know yet. I only just figured it out myself.'

'Interesting,' Curtis says. He turns to Liz. 'Where do you think you are, Lizzie?'

Liz clears her throat. Her parents call her Lizzie. All at once and for no apparent reason, she misses them desperately.

Curtis looks at her with concern. 'Are you all right?'

'No, I . . .' Liz returns the conversation to solid ground. 'When is the new album out?'

Curtis eats one french fry. And then another. 'Never,' he says.

'The band broke up?' Liz has always read rumors of a possible Machine split, but they have never come to pass.

'That's one way of saying it,' Curtis replies.

'What happened?' Liz asks.

'I quit.'

'But why? You guys were so great!' For her birthday, she has tickets to their concert in Boston. 'I don't understand.'

Curtis pushes up the left sleeve of his white pajama top, revealing his inner forearm. Deep tracklike scars, purplish bruises, and crusty wounds run from his inner elbow to his wrist. There is a quarter-inch hole near the crease separating Curtis's biceps from his forearm. The hole is completely black. Liz thinks his arm looks dead. 'Because I was a fool, Lizzie my lass,' Curtis says.

'Liz?' Thandi says.

Liz just stares dumbly at Curtis's arm.

'Liz, are you okay?' Thandi asks.

'I'm . . .' Liz begins. She hates looking at the rotten arm, but she can't stop looking at it either.

'Good Lord, would you put that arm away?' Thandi orders Curtis. 'You're making her sick. Honestly, Liz, it isn't any worse than the hole in my head.'

'Hole in your head?' Curtis asks. 'Could I see it?'

'Of course.' Flattered, Thandi forgets all about Liz and begins to raise her braids.

The thought of seeing the hole and the arm at the same time is too much for Liz. 'Excuse me,' she says.

Liz runs outside onto the main deck of the ship. All around her, older people in various styles of white pajamas are playing shuffleboard. She leans over the ship's railing and stares into the water. The water is too far away for her to see her reflection in it, but if she leans far enough over, she can sort of see her shadow—an indistinct, small darkness in the middle of an expanse of blue.

I am dreaming, she thinks, and any moment, my alarm clock will sound, and I will wake up.

Wake up, wake up, wake up, she wills herself. Liz pinches herself on the arm as hard as she can. 'Ow,' she says. She slaps herself across the face. Nothing. And then she slaps herself again. Still nothing. She closes her eyes as tightly as she can and then snaps them open again, hoping to find herself back in her own bed on Carroll Drive in Medford, Massachusetts.

Liz starts to panic. Tears form in her eyes; she furiously brushes them away with her hand.

I am fifteen years old, a mature person with a learner's permit, three months away from an actual driver's license, she thinks. I am too old to be having nightmares.

She screws her eyes shut and screams, 'MOM! MOM! I'M HAVING A NIGHTMARE!' Liz waits for her mother to wake her up.

Any moment.

Any moment, Liz's mother should arrive at her bedside with a comforting glass of water.

Any moment.

Liz opens one eye. She is still on the ship's main deck, where people have begun to stare.

'Young lady,' says an old man with horn-rimmed glasses and the air of a substitute teacher, 'you are being disruptive.'

Liz sits down by the railing and buries her head in her hands. She takes a deep breath and tells herself to calm down. She decides that the best strategy will be to try to remember as many details of the dream as possible so she can tell her mother about it in the morning.

But how had the dream started? Liz racks her brain. It is odd to try to recall a dream while one is still having the dream. Oh yes! Liz remembers now.

The dream began at her house on Carroll Drive.

She was riding her bike to the Cambridgeside Galleria. She was supposed to meet her best friend, Zooey, who needed to buy a dress for the prom. (Liz herself had not been invited yet.) Liz could remember arriving at the intersection by the mall, across the street from the bicycle racks. Out of nowhere, a taxicab came speeding toward her.

She could remember the sensation of flying through the air, which seemed to last an eternity. She could remember feeling reckless, happy, and doomed, all at the same time. She could remember thinking, I am above gravity.

Liz sighs. Looking at it objectively, she supposes she died in the dream. Liz wonders what it means when you die in your dreams, and she resolves to ask her mom in the morning. All at once, she wonders if going to sleep again is the answer. Maybe if she can just manage to fall asleep, the next time she wakes up, everything will be back to normal. She feels grateful to Thandi for making her memorize their cabin number.

As Liz walks briskly back across the deck, she notices an SS *Nile* life preserver. Liz smiles at the ship's name. The week before, she had been studying ancient Egypt in Mrs. Early's world history class. While the lesson was entertaining enough (war, pestilence, plague, murder), Liz considered the whole pyramid thing a real waste of time and resources. In Liz's opinion, a pyramid was really the same as a pine box or a Quaker oats container; by the time pharaoh got to enjoy his pyramid, he'd be dead anyway. Liz thought the Egyptians should have lived in the pyramids and been buried in their huts (or wherever it was that ancient Egyptian people had lived).

At the end of the unit, Mrs. Early read a poem about Egypt which began, 'I met a traveler from an antique land.' For some reason, the line gave Liz chills, the pleasurable kind, and she kept repeating it to herself all day: 'I met a traveler from an antique land; I met a traveler from an antique land.' Liz supposes Mrs. Early's lesson is the reason she dreams of a ship called the SS *Nile*.

In Memory of
Elizabeth Marie Hall

Night after night, Liz goes to sleep, but she never wakes up in Medford; time passes, but she doesn't know how much. Despite a thorough search of the boat, neither she nor Thandi can unearth a single calendar, television, telephone, computer, or even radio. The only thing Liz knows for sure is that she is no longer bald—a quarter inch of hair covers her entire head. How long, she wonders, does hair take to grow? How long does a dream have to last before it's just life?

Liz is lying in her bed, staring at the upper bunk, when she notices the sound of Thandi sobbing.

'Thandi,' Liz asks, craning her neck upward, 'are you all right?'

Thandi's crying intensifies. Finally, she is able to speak. 'I m-m-miss my boyfriend.'

Liz hands Thandi a tissue. Although the *Nile* lacks modern

electronic devices, tissue abounds. 'What's his name?'

'Reginald Christopher Doral Monmount Harris the Third,' Thandi says, 'but I call him Slim even though he's anything but. You have a guy, Liz?'

Liz takes a moment to contemplate this question. Her romantic life has been sadly lacking to this point. When she was in second grade, Raphael Annuncio brought her a box of conversational hearts on Valentine's Day. Although it seemed a promising gesture, Raphael asked her to return the candy the next morning. It was too late: she had already eaten all but one of the hearts (U R 2 SWEET).

And then in eighth grade, she invented a boyfriend to make herself appear more worldly to the popular girls in school. Liz claimed she met Steve Detroit (that was what she called him!) when she was visiting her cousin at Andover. Steve Detroit may have been a fictional boy, but Liz made him a real bastard. He cheated on Liz, called her fat, made her do his homework, and even borrowed ten dollars without paying it back.

In the summer before ninth grade, Liz met a boy at camp. A counselor named Josh, who once sort of held her elbow at a bonfire, a move which Liz found inexplicably delightful and astonishing. Upon returning home, Liz wrote him a passionate letter, but sadly he did not respond. Later, Liz would wonder if Josh had even realized he was holding her elbow. Maybe he had just thought the elbow was part of the armrest?

To date, her most serious relationship was with Edward, a cross-country runner. They were in the same math class. Liz had ended the relationship in January, before the start of the spring season. She couldn't bear to attend even one more meet. Cross-country, in Liz's opinion, was quite possibly the most boring sport on earth. Liz wonders if Edward would care if she were dead.

'So, Liz,' Thandi asks, 'do you have a boyfriend, or not?'

'Not really,' Liz admits.

'You're lucky. I don't think Slim misses me at all.'

Liz doesn't answer. She doesn't know if she is lucky.

She gets out of bed and looks at herself in the mirror over the bureau. Except for her current haircut, she isn't terrible looking, and yet the boys in her class never seem particularly interested. With a sigh, Liz examines the new hair that is growing on her head. She cranes her neck, trying to see what the back looks like. And that's when she sees it: a long row of stitches sewn in a C-shaped arc over her left ear. The wound is beginning to heal, and hair is beginning to grow over the stitches. But they are still there. Liz gingerly touches the stitches with her hand. The stitches feel like they should hurt, but they don't.

'Thandi, have you seen these before?'

'Yeah, they been there as long as you been here.'

Liz marvels that she hadn't noticed them. 'It's odd, isn't it,' she asks, 'that you should have a hole in the back of your head, and I should have these stitches over my ear, and yet we're both fine? I mean, these stitches don't hurt at all.'

'You don't remember how you got them?'

Liz thinks for a moment. 'In the dream,' she begins and then stops. 'I think I may have been in this sort of a . . . this sort of a bicycle accident.'

Suddenly, Liz needs to sit down. She feels cold and breathless. 'Thandi,' Liz says, 'I want to know how you got the hole in your head.'

'It's like I told you. I was shot.'

'Yes, but what happened? Specifically, I mean.'

'Best I can recall, I was walking down my street with Slim. We live in D.C., by the way. This crazy bullet comes out of nowhere. Slim's yelling at me to duck, and then he's screaming, "SHE'S BLEEDING! OH LORD, SHE'S BLEEDING!" Next thing I know, you're waking me up on this very boat, asking me where you are.' Thandi twirls one of her braids around her finger. 'You know, Liz, at first I didn't remember everything, either, but then I started to remember more and more.'

Liz nods. 'Are you sure you aren't dreaming all of this?'

'I know that's your opinion of the matter, but I know I'm not dreaming. Dreaming feels like dreaming, and this doesn't feel like dreaming.'

'But it doesn't seem possible, does it? You getting shot in the head, and me in a serious bicycle crash, and both of us walking around perfectly fine, as if nothing happened.'

Thandi shakes her head, but chooses not to speak.

'Plus, why would Curtis Jest be here? Isn't meeting a famous rock star the sort of thing that only happens in a dream?' Liz asks.

'But, Liz, you know those marks on his arm?'

'Yes.'

'I had this cousin in Baltimore called Shelly. Shelly had marks sort of like that. They're the sort of marks you get when you're using—'

Liz interrupts Thandi. 'I don't want to know about that. Curtis

Jest is nothing like your cousin Shelly from Baltimore. Nothing at all!'

'Fine, but don't get mad at me. You're the one bringing this stuff up.'

'I'm sorry, Thandi,' Liz apologizes. 'I'm just trying to figure everything out.'

Thandi lets out a long, plaintive sigh. 'Girl, you are in denial,' she says.

Before Liz has a chance to ask Thandi what she means, someone pushes a large beige envelope under the cabin door. Grateful for the distraction, Liz retrieves the envelope. It is addressed in deep blue ink:

Passager Elizabeth M. Hall
Formerly of Medford, Massachusetts, in
the United States of America
Currently of the SS Nile, Cabin 130002,
Bottom Bunk

Liz opens the door. She looks up and down the hallway, but no one is there.

Returning to the bottom bunk, Liz looks in the envelope. Inside, she finds a plain card with a vellum overlay and an odd hexagonal coin with a round hole in the center. The coin reminds Liz of the subway tokens back home. The coin is embossed with the words ONE ETERNIM on the front and OFFICIAL CURRENCY OF ELSEWHERE on the back. The card appears to be an invitation, but the occasion isn't specified:

Dear Passager Hall,
Your presence is requested:
Observation Deck
Binoculars #219
Today
NOW!

'Who ever heard of sending an invitation to something that's happening "now"? You can't help but be late,' Liz says as she shows the invitation to Thandi.

'Actually, Liz, you can't help but be on time. "Now" being a relative term and all,' Thandi says.

'Do you want to come?' Liz asks.

'It's probably best you go alone.'

'Suit yourself.' Liz is still annoyed with Thandi and is secretly glad to be by herself.

'Besides, I've already been,' Thandi admits.

'When were you there without me?' Liz asks.

'Sometime,' Thandi says vaguely. 'Don't matter.'

Liz shakes her head. As she sees it, she is already late and doesn't have time to further question Thandi.

On her way out the door, Liz turns to face Thandi. 'Heroin,' says Liz. 'That's what those marks on Curtis's arm were from, right?'

Thandi nods. 'I thought you didn't know.'

'In the magazines, there were always rumors that Curtis Jest was a junkie,' Liz says, 'but you can't believe everything you read.'

The Observation Deck is on the top floor of the ship. Although

26

Liz and Thandi have explored the *Nile* extensively, they have never gone all the way to the top. (At least not together, Liz thinks.) Now Liz wonders *why* they never went up. All at once, Liz needs to get there. She senses that when she reaches the Observation Deck, something definitive will happen.

Liz races up the many flights of stairs that separate her cabin from the Observation Deck. She finds herself chanting the line from the poem Mrs. Early read in class: 'I met a traveler from an antique land; I met a traveler from an antique land; I met a traveler from an antique land.' When Liz finally reaches the top, she is covered in sweat and out of breath.

The Observation Deck consists of a long row of binoculars, the kind that resemble stick-figure men without arms, or parking meters. Each pair of binoculars is coupled with an uncomfortable-looking metal stool. The people using the binoculars are consistently rapt, although their individual reactions differ wildly. Some laugh; some cry; some laugh and cry at the same time; some simply stare straight ahead, blank expressions on their faces.

The binoculars are labeled sequentially. Filled with equal parts fear and curiosity, Liz locates Binoculars #219 and sits on the metal stool. She removes the strange coin from her pocket and places it in the slot. She puts her eyes up to the binoculars just as the lenses click open. What can almost be described as a 3-D movie is playing.

The movie is set at a church. Liz recognizes it as the one she attended whenever her mother felt the intermittent need to 'enhance Liz's spiritual life.' In the back pews, Liz sees several kids from her high school dressed in black. As the camera moves forward through the church, Liz sees other, older people; people she only knows from long-forgotten holiday meals and dinner parties viewed from upstairs after her bedtime. Yes, these are her relatives and her parents' friends. Finally, the camera stops at the front of the church. Liz's mother, father, and brother are sitting in the front row. Her mother wears no makeup and clutches her father by the hand. Her brother wears a navy blue suit that is already too short for him.

Dr. Frederick, her high school principal and a man Liz has never spoken to personally, stands at the pulpit. 'A straight-A student,' says Dr. Frederick in what Liz recognizes as the voice he uses for assemblies, 'Elizabeth Marie Hall was a credit to her parents and her school.' Liz laughs. Although her grades ranged from decent to very good, she never made straight A's. Mainly, she made B's, except in math and science.

'But what can we learn from the death of a person so young, with so much potential?' Dr. Frederick bangs on the lectern with his fist for emphasis. 'What we can learn is the importance of traffic safety.' At this point, Liz's father erupts in an explosion of breathless, hysterical sobs. In her whole life, Liz has never once seen him cry like that.

'In memory of Elizabeth Marie Hall,' Dr. Frederick continues, 'I challenge you all to look both ways before you cross the street, to wear a helmet when riding a bicycle, to fasten your seat belts, to only purchase automobiles that include passenger-side airbags . . .' Dr. Frederick shows no signs of stopping. What a windbag, Liz thinks.

Liz pans the binoculars to the left. Beside the lectern, she notices a rectangular white lacquer box with tacky pink roses carved into its side. At this point, Liz has a fairly good idea what, or rather who, will be in the box. Still, she knows she must see for herself. Liz peers over the lid: a lifeless girl in a blond wig and a brown velvet dress lies in a bed of white satin. I've always hated that dress, Liz thinks. She sits back on her uncomfortable metal stool and sighs. She knows what she had, until now, only suspected: she is dead. She is dead and, for the moment anyway, she feels nothing.

Liz takes one last look in the binoculars, checking to make sure that the people who should be at her funeral are there. Edward the cross-country runner is there, manfully blowing his nose on his sleeve. Her English teacher is there, and so is Personal Fitness. She is pleasantly surprised to see World History. But what happened to Algebra II and Biology? Liz wonders. (Those were her favorite subjects.) And she can't seem to find her best friend anywhere. Hadn't it been Zooey's fault she was at the mall to begin with? Where the hell is Zooey? Disgusted, Liz leaves the binoculars before her time is up. She has seen enough.

I am dead, Liz thinks. And then she says it aloud to hear how it sounds: 'I am dead. *Dead.*'

It is a strange thing being dead, because her body doesn't feel dead at all. Her body feels the same as it always has.

As Liz walks down the long row of binoculars, she spots Curtis Jest. Using only one eye, he is looking in his binoculars with decidedly tepid interest. His other eye spots Liz immediately.

'Hello, Lizzie. How's the afterlife treating you?' Curtis asks.

Liz tries to shrug nonchalantly. Although she does not know exactly what 'the afterlife' entails, she is fairly certain of one thing: she will never see her parents, her brother, or her friends again. In a way, it feels more like she is still alive and the only guest at the collective funeral for everyone she has ever known. She chooses to respond with 'It's boring,' even though that answer doesn't come close to expressing what she feels.

'And the funeral, how was that?' asks Curtis.

'It was mainly an occasion for my high school principal to discuss traffic safety.'

'Traffic safety, eh? Sounds divine.' Curtis cocks his head, slightly puzzled.

'And they said I was a 'straight-A student,' ' Liz adds, 'which I'm not.'

'Don't you watch the news? All young people become perfect students when they kick the bucket. It's a rule.'

Liz wonders if her death made the local news. Does anyone care if a fifteen-year-old girl gets hit by a car?

'The Great Jimi Hendrix said, 'Everyone loves you when you're dead: once you're dead, you're made for life.' Or something like that. But he's probably before your time.'

'I know who he is,' Liz says. 'The guitar player.'

'I beg your pardon, madam.' Curtis mimes tipping his hat. 'Care to have a look at my funeral, then?' Curtis asks.

Liz isn't sure she is up to looking at anyone else's funeral, but she doesn't want to seem impolite. She looks through Curtis's binoculars. Curtis's funeral is far more elaborate than Liz's: the other members of Machine are there; a famous singer sings his most famous song with lyrics especially rewritten for the occasion; a celebrated underwear model sobs in the front row; and, bizarrely, a juggling bear stands on Curtis's coffin.

'What's with the bear?' Liz asks.

'The bear was supposed to be in our next video. His name is Bartholomew, and I was told he is the best bear in the business. One of the guys in the band probably thought I would like it.'

Liz steps away from the binoculars. 'How did you die, Curtis?'

'Apparent drug overdose, I suppose.'

'Apparent?' Liz asks.

'No doubt, that's what they said on the news: "Curtis Jest, lead singer of the band Machine, died of an apparent drug overdose early Sunday morning at his residence in Los Angeles. He was thirty years old." It's a great tragedy, you see.' Curtis laughs. 'And you, Lizzie? Do you know now?'

'Bicycle accident.'

'Ah, that explains the traffic-safety-themed funeral.'

'I guess. My mom was always trying to get me to wear a helmet,' says Liz.

'Mums always know best.'

Liz smiles. A moment later, she is surprised to find tears falling from her eyes. She quickly brushes them away with her hand, but they are soon replaced with fresh stock.

'Here,' says Curtis, holding out his pajama sleeve for Liz to wipe her eyes on.

Liz accepts the sleeve. She notices that Curtis's scarred arm is healing. 'Thank you,' she says. 'Your arm looks better, by the way.'

Curtis pulls down his pajama sleeve. 'My youngest sister is your age,' Curtis says. 'Looks a bit like you, too.'

'We're dead, you know? We're all dead. And we're never going to see any of them ever again,' Liz cries.

'Who knows, Lizzie? Perhaps we will.'

'Easy for you to say. You chose this.' As soon as the words escape her mouth, Liz regrets them.

Curtis waits a moment before he responds. 'I was a drug addict. I didn't want to die.'

'I'm sorry.'

Curtis nods without really looking at Liz.

'I'm really sorry,' she says. 'It was a stupid thing for me to say. I only thought it, because a lot of your songs are kind of, well, dark. But I still shouldn't assume things.'

'Apology accepted. It's a good thing to know how to apologize properly. Very few people know how to do it.' Curtis smiles, and Liz returns his smile. 'And the truth is, some days I did want to die, maybe a little. But not most days.'

Liz thinks about asking him if he still wants drugs now that he's dead, but she decides the question isn't appropriate. 'People will be really sad you're gone,' Liz says.

'Will they?'

'Well,' she says, 'I'm sad you're gone.'

'But I'm where you are. So to you, I'm not gone, am I?'

'No, I guess not.' Liz laughs. It feels strange to laugh. How can anything be funny now?

'Do you think we'll be on this boat forever? I mean, is this all there is?' Liz asks.

'I suspect not, Lizzie.'

'But how do you know?'

'Perhaps my mind's playing tricks on me,' says Curtis, 'but I think I can see the shore, love.'

Liz stands to see over the binoculars. In the distance, she can see what appears to be land. The sight momentarily comforts her. If you have to be dead, it is better to be somewhere, anywhere, than nowhere at all.

Part II: The Book of the Dead

Welcome to Elsewhere

We're here!' Thandi is looking out the upper porthole when Liz enters the cabin. She jumps down from the top bunk and throws her solid arms around Liz, spinning her about the cabin until both girls are out of breath.

Liz sits down and gasps for air. 'How can you be so happy when we're . . . ?' Her voice trails off.

'Dead?' Thandi smiles a little. 'So you finally figured it out.'

'I just got back from my funeral, but I think I sort of knew before.'

Thandi nods solemnly. 'It takes as long as it takes,' she says. 'My funeral was awful, thanks for asking. They had me made up like a clown. I can't even talk about what they did to my hair.' Thandi lifts up her braids. In the mirror, she examines the hole in the back of her head. 'It's definitely getting smaller,' she decides before lowering her braids.

'Aren't you at all sad?' Liz asks.

'No point in being sad that I can see. I can't change anything. And I'm tired of being in this little room, Liz, no offense.'

An announcement comes over the ship's PA system: 'This is your captain speaking. I hope you've enjoyed your passage. On behalf of the crew of the SS *Nile*, welcome to Elsewhere. The local temperature is 67 degrees with partly sunny skies and a westerly breeze. The local time is 3:48 p.m. All passagers must now disembark. This is the last and only stop.'

'Don't you wonder what it's like out there?' Liz asks.

'The captain just said. It's warm with a breeze.'

'No, not the weather. I meant, everything else.'

'Not really. It is what it is, and all the wondering in the world isn't gonna change it.' Thandi holds out her hand to help Liz off the bed. 'You coming?'

Liz shakes her head. 'The ship's probably super crowded. I think I'll wait here a bit, just until the halls clear out.'

Thandi sits next to Liz on the bed. 'I'm in no particular rush.'

'No, you go on ahead,' says Liz. 'I want to be by myself.'

Thandi looks into Liz's eyes. 'Don't you stay in here forever.'

'I won't. I promise.'

Thandi nods. She is almost out the door when Liz calls out to her, 'Why do you think they put us together anyway?'

'Beats me.' Thandi shrugs. 'We were probably the only two sixteen-year-old girls who died of acute head traumas that day.'

'I'm fifteen,' Liz reminds her.

'Guess that was the best they could do.' Thandi pulls Liz into a hug. 'It was certainly nice meeting you, Liz. Maybe I'll see you again someday.'

Liz wants to say something to acknowledge the profound experience that she and Thandi have just shared, but she can't find the right words. 'Yeah, see you,' Liz replies.

As Thandi closes the door, Liz has the impulse to call out and ask her to stay. Thandi is now her only friend, except for Curtis Jest. (And Liz isn't even sure if she can count Curtis Jest a friend.) With Thandi gone, Liz feels more alone and wretched than she has ever felt before.

Liz lies down on the bottom bunk. All around her, she can hear the sounds of people leaving their cabins and walking through the ship's halls. Liz decides to wait until she can't hear any more people and only then will she venture from her cabin. In between doors opening and closing, she listens to snippets of conversation.

A man says, 'It's a little embarrassing to only have these nightgowns to wear . . .'

And a woman, 'I hope there's a decent hotel . . .'

And another woman, 'Do you think I'll see Hubie there? Oh, how I have missed him!'

Liz wonders who 'Hubie' is. She guesses he is probably dead like all the people on the *Nile*, dead like she is. Maybe being dead isn't so bad if you are really old, she thinks, because, as far as she can tell, most dead people *are* really old. So the chance of meeting new people your own age is quite good. And all the other dead people you knew from before you died might even be in the new place, Elsewhere, or whatever it was called. And maybe if you got old enough, you'd know more dead people than live ones, so dying would be a good thing, or at least wouldn't be so bad. As Liz sees it, for the aged, death isn't much different than retiring to Florida.

But Liz is fifteen (almost sixteen), and she doesn't personally know any dead people. Except for herself and the people on the trip, of course. To Liz, the prospect of being dead seems terribly lonely.

On the drive over to the Elsewhere pier, Betty Bloom, a woman prone to talking to herself, remarks, 'I wish I had met Elizabeth even once. Then I could say, 'Remember that time we met?' As it is, I have to say, 'I'm your grandmother. We never met, on account of my untimely death from breast cancer.' And frankly, cancer is no way to begin a conversation. In fact, I think it might be better not to mention cancer at all. Suffice it to say, I died. At the very least, we both have that in common.' Betty sighs. A car honks at her. Instead of speeding up, Betty smiles, waves, and allows the car to pass. 'Yes, I am perfectly content to be driving at the speed I'm driving. If you wish to go faster, by all means go,' she adds.

'I do wish I had more time to prepare for Elizabeth's arrival. It's odd to think of myself as someone's grandmother, and I don't feel very grandmotherly at all. I dislike baking, all cooking actually, and doilies and housecoats. And although I like children very much, I'm not very good with them, I'm afraid.

'For Olivia's sake, I promise not to be strict or judgmental. And I promise not to treat Elizabeth like a child. And I promise to treat her like an equal. And I promise to be supportive. And I won't ask too many questions. In return, I hope she'll like me a little bit, despite anything Olivia may have told her.' For a moment, Betty falls silent and wonders how Olivia, her only child, is doing.

Arriving at the pier, Betty checks her reflection in the rearview mirror and is surprised by what she sees. 'Not quite old, not quite young. Very strange, indeed.'

An hour passes. And then another. The halls grow quiet and then silent. Liz begins to hatch a plan. Maybe she could just be a stowaway? Eventually the boat would have to make a return trip, right? And if Liz just stays on it, maybe she could simply return to her old life. Maybe it's really that easy, Liz thinks. Maybe when she heard stories of people who had had near-death experiences, people who had flatlined and then come back, those 'lucky' people were not lucky at all. They were the ones who knew enough to stay on the boat.

Liz imagines her homecoming. Everyone will say, 'It's a miracle!' All the newspapers will cover it: LOCAL GIRL BACK FROM DEAD; CLAIMS DEATH IS CRUISE, NOT WHITE LIGHT, TUNNEL. LIZ will get a book deal (*Dead Girl* by Liz Hall) *and* a TV movie (*Determined to Live: The Elizabeth M. Hall Story*) *and* an appearance on *Oprah* to promote both.

Liz sees the doorknob move, and the door begins to open. Without really thinking about it, she hides under the bed. From her position, she can see a boy of around her brother's age, dressed in a white captain's costume with gold epaulets and a matching captain's hat. He sits himself on the lower bunk and appears to take no notice of Liz.

The boy's only movement is the slight swinging of his legs. Liz notices that his feet barely reach the floor. She has a perfect view of the soles of his shoes. Someone has written *L* on the left one and *R* on the right one in black marker.

After a few minutes, the boy speaks. 'I was waiting for you to introduce yourself,' he says with an unusually mature voice for a child, 'but I don't have all day.'

Liz doesn't answer.

'I am the Captain,' the boy says, 'and you are not supposed to be in here.'

Liz still doesn't answer. She holds her breath and tries not to make a single sound.

'Yes, girl under the bed. The Captain is speaking to you.'

'The Captain of what?' Liz whispers.

'The Captain of the SS *Nile*, of course.'

'You look a little young to be the captain.'

'I assure you my experience and qualifications are exemplary. I have been the Captain for nearly one hundred years.'

What a comedian, Liz thinks. 'How old are you?'

'I am seven,' the Captain says with dignity.

'Isn't seven a bit young to be a captain?'

The Captain nods his head. 'Yes,' he concedes, 'I must now take naps in the afternoon. I will probably retire next year.'

'I want to make the return trip,' Liz says.

'These boats only go one way.'

Liz peers out from under the bed. 'That doesn't make sense. They have to get back somehow.'

'I don't make the rules,' says the Captain.

'What rules? I'm dead!'

'If you think your death gives you free rein to act as you please, you are wrong,' says the Captain. 'Dead wrong,' he adds a moment later. He laughs at his bad pun and then abruptly stops. 'Let's suspend disbelief for a moment, and say you managed to take this boat back to Earth. What do you think would happen?'

Liz pulls herself out from under the bed. 'I suppose I'd go back to my old life, right?'

The Captain shakes his head. 'No. You wouldn't have a body to go back to. You'd be a ghost.'

'Well, maybe that wouldn't be so bad.'

'Trust me. I know people who've tried, and it's no kind of life. You end up crazy, and everyone you love ends up crazy, too. Take a piece of advice: get off the boat.'

Liz's eyes are welling up with tears again. Dying certainly makes a person weepy, she thinks as she wipes her eyes with the back of her hand.

The Captain pulls a handkerchief out of his pocket and hands it to her. The handkerchief is made from the softest, thinnest cotton, more like paper than cloth, and is embroidered with the words *The Captain*. Liz blows her nose in it. Her father carries handkerchiefs. And the memory necessitates another nose blow.

'Don't cry. It's not so bad here,' the Captain says.

Liz shakes her head. 'It's the dust from under the bed. It's getting in my eyes.' She returns the handkerchief to the Captain.

'Keep it,' says the Captain. 'You'll probably need it again.' He stands with the perfect posture of a career military man, but his head only comes up to Liz's chest. 'I trust you'll be leaving in the next five minutes,' he says. 'You don't want to stay.' And with that, he quietly closes the cabin door behind him.

Liz considers what the strange little boy has said. As much as she longs to be with her family and her friends, she doesn't want to be a ghost. She certainly doesn't want to cause more pain to the people she loves. She knows there is only one thing to do.

Liz looks out the porthole one last time. The sun has almost set, and she passingly wonders if it is the same sun they have at home.

The only person on the dock is Betty Bloom. Although Liz has never seen Betty before, something about the woman reminds Liz of her own mother. Betty waves to Liz and begins walking toward her with purposeful, even strides.

'Welcome, Elizabeth! I've been waiting such a long time to meet you.' The woman pulls Liz into a tight embrace that Liz attempts to wiggle out of. 'How like Olivia.'

'How do you know my mother?' Liz demands.

'I'm her mother, your Grandma Betty, but you never met me. I died before you were born.' Grandma Betty embraces Liz again. 'You were named for me; my full name's Elizabeth, too, but I've always been Betty.'

'But how is that possible? How can you be my grandmother when you look the same age as my mother?' Liz asks.

'Welcome to Elsewhere.' Grandma Betty laughs, pointing matter-of-factly to the large banner that hangs over the pier.

'I don't understand.'

'Here, no one gets older, everyone gets younger. But don't worry, they'll explain all of that at your acclimation appointment.'

'I'm getting younger? But it took me so long to get to fifteen!'

'Don't worry, darling, it all works out in the end. You're going to love it here.'

Understandably, Liz isn't so sure.

A Long Drive Home

In Grandma Betty's red convertible, Liz just stares out the window and lets her grandmother do all the talking.

'Do you like architecture?' Grandma Betty asks.

Liz shrugs. In all honesty, she has never put much thought into the subject.

'Out my window, you'll see a library built by Frank Lloyd Wright. People who know these things say it's better than any of the buildings he built on Earth. And Elizabeth, it's not just buildings. You'll find new works here by many of your favorite artists. Books, paintings, music, whatever you're into! I just went to an exhibit of new paintings by Picasso, if you can believe it!' Liz thinks Grandma Betty's enthusiasm seems forced, as if she's trying to convince a reluctant child to eat broccoli.

'I met Curtis Jest on the boat,' Liz says quietly.

'Who's he?'

'He's the lead singer of Machine.'

'I don't think I've ever heard of them. But then, I died a while ago, so that's no surprise. Maybe he'll record something new here?'

Liz shrugs again.

'Of course, some artists don't continue here,' Grandma Betty goes on. 'I suppose just one life of art can be quite enough. Artists are never the happiest folks, are they? Do you know the film star Marilyn Monroe? Well, she's a psychiatrist. Or rather she was, until she got too young to practice. My neighbor Phyllis used to go to her. Oh, Elizabeth, and straight ahead? The funny, tall building? That's the Registry. That's where you'll have your acclimation appointment tomorrow.'

Liz looks out the car window. So this is Elsewhere, she thinks. Liz sees a place that looks like almost any other place on Earth. She thinks it is cruel how ordinary it is, how much it resembles real life. There are buildings, houses, stores, roads, cars, bridges, people, trees, flowers, grass, lakes, rivers, beaches, air, stars, and skies. How entirely unremarkable, she thinks. Elsewhere could have been a walk to the next town or an hour's ride in the car or an overnight plane trip. As they continue to drive, Liz notices that all the roads are curved and that even when it seems like they're driving straight, they're actually going in a sort of circle.

After a while, Grandma Betty realizes that Liz isn't keeping up her end of the conversation. 'Am I talking too much? I know I have a tendency to—'

Liz interrupts. 'What did you mean when you said I was getting younger?'

Grandma Betty looks at Liz. 'Are you sure you want to know now?'

Liz nods.

'Everyone here ages backward from the day they died. When I got here, I was fifty. I've been here for just over sixteen years, so now I'm thirty-four. For most older people, Lizzie, this is a good thing. I imagine it isn't quite as appealing when one is your age.'

Liz takes a moment to absorb Grandma Betty's words. I will never turn sixteen, she thinks. 'What happens when I get to zero?' Liz asks.

'Well, you become a baby again. And when you're seven days old, you and all the other babies are sent down the River, back to Earth to be born anew. It's called the Release.'

'So I'll only be here fifteen years, and then I go back to Earth to start all over again?'

'You'll be here almost sixteen years,' Grandma Betty corrects her, 'but basically, yes.'

Liz can't believe how unfair this is. If it isn't bad enough that she died before getting to do anything fun, now she will have to repeat her whole life in reverse until she becomes a stupid, sniveling baby again.

'So I'll never be an adult?' Liz asks.

'I wouldn't look at it that way, Liz. Your mind still acquires experience and memories even while your body—'

Liz explodes, 'I'LL NEVER GO TO COLLEGE OR GET MARRIED OR GET BIG BOOBS OR LIVE ON MY OWN OR

FALL IN LOVE OR GET MY DRIVER'S LICENSE OR ANY-
THING? I CAN'T BELIEVE THIS!'

Grandma Betty pulls the car to the side of the road.
'You'll see,' she says, patting Liz on the hand. 'It isn't all that
bad.'

'Not all that bad? How the hell could it get any worse? I'm fifteen, and I'm dead. Dead!' For a minute, no one speaks.

Suddenly, Grandma Betty claps her hands together: 'I've just
had the most marvelous idea, Elizabeth. You have your learner's
permit, right?'

Liz nods.

'Why don't you drive us back to the house?'

Liz nods again. Although she is justifiably upset by the turn of
events, she doesn't want to pass up an opportunity to drive.
After all, she'll probably never get her driver's license in this stupid place, and who knows how many months until they'll take
away her learner's permit, too. Liz opens the passenger door
and gets out as Grandma Betty slides across the bench seat to
the passenger side.

'Do you know how to maneuver this kind of transmission? My
car's a bit of a dinosaur, I'm afraid,' says Grandma Betty.

'I can do everything except parallel parking and three-point
turns,' Liz answers calmly. 'We were supposed to cover those
next in driver's ed, but unfortunately for me, I croaked.'

The route to Grandma Betty's house is simple enough, and
aside from the occasional direction, the ride is silent. Although
she has plenty to say, Grandma Betty doesn't want to distract
Liz from her driving. Liz isn't in the mood for conversation anyway and she lets her mind wander. Of course, a wandering

mind is not always advisable for the recently deceased and is nearly never advisable for the beginning driver.

Liz thinks about why it took her so long to figure out she was dead. Other people, like Curtis and Thandi, seemed to realize immediately, or soon thereafter. She feels like a real dunce. At school, Liz always prided herself on being a person who caught on quickly, a fast learner. But here was concrete evidence that she is not as fast as she thinks.

'Elizabeth, darling,' says Grandma Betty, 'you may want to slow down a bit.'

'Fine,' says Liz, glancing at the speedometer, which reads seventy-five miles per hour. She didn't realize she was driving so fast and eases up a bit on the gas pedal.

How can I be dead? Liz wonders to herself. Aren't I too young to be dead? When dead people are her age, they're usually little kids with cancer or some equally horrible and abstract disease. Dead little kids get free trips and meet world-famous pop stars. She wonders if a cruise and Curtis Jest counted.

When Liz was a freshman, two seniors had been killed drinking and driving just before the prom. The school had given them full-page, full-color tributes in the yearbook. Liz wonders if she will receive such a tribute. Unless her parents pay for it, she doubts it. Both boys had been on the football team, which had won the Massachusetts state championship that year. Liz did not play football, was only a sophomore, and had died by herself. (People always find dying in groups more tragic.) She steps on the gas pedal a little harder.

'Elizabeth,' says Grandma Betty, 'the house is the next

exit. I suggest slowing down and easing the car into the right lane.'

Without a glance in the rearview mirror, Liz moves into the right lane. She cuts off a black sports car and has to speed up to keep the car from crashing into her back end.

'Elizabeth, did you see that car?' asks Grandma Betty.

'It's under control,' says Liz tightly. So what if I'm a bad driver? Liz thinks to herself. What difference does it make anyway? It's not like I'm going to get myself killed. You can't get deader than dead, can you?

'This is the exit. Are you sure you're all right to drive?'

'I'm fine,' says Liz. Without slowing down, she maneuvers the car awkwardly toward the exit.

'You might want to slow down; the exit can be somewhat tricky to—'

'I'm fine!' Liz yells.

'WATCH OUT!'

At that moment, Liz drives the car into the exit's concrete retaining wall. The car is a heavy old beast and makes an impressive noise upon contact.

'Are you hurt?' asks Grandma Betty.

Liz doesn't answer. Staring at the old car's front end, Liz can't help but laugh. The car has sustained almost no damage. A single dent, that's all. A miracle, thinks Liz bitterly. If only people were as sturdy as cars.

'Elizabeth, are you all right?' asks Grandma Betty.

'No,' Liz answers. 'I'm dead, or haven't you heard?'

'I meant, are you hurt?'

Liz strokes the remains of the stitches over her ear. She wonders who she should see about removing the stitches. She had stitches once before (a rollerskating accident at age nine, her most serious injury until recently) and she knows that wounds don't fully heal until stitches are removed. All at once, Liz doesn't want to have the stitches removed. She finds this tiny piece of string strangely comforting. It is her last piece of Earth and the only evidence that she was ever there at all.

'Are you hurt?' Grandma Betty repeats the question, looking at Liz with concern.

'What difference would it make?'

'Well,' says Grandma Betty, 'if you were hurt, I would take you to a healing center.'

'People get hurt here?'

'Yes, although everything eventually heals when one ages backward.'

'So nothing matters here, does it? I mean, nothing counts. Everything is just erased. We're all getting younger and stupider, and that's it.' Liz wants to cry, but not in front of Betty, whom she doesn't even know.

'You could look at things that way, I suppose. But in my opinion, that would be a very boring and limited point of view. I would hope you haven't embraced such a bleak outlook before you've even been here a day.' Cupping Liz's chin in her hand, Grandma Betty turns Liz's head so that she can see directly into her eyes. 'Were you trying to kill us back there?'

'Could I?'

Grandma Betty shakes her head. 'No, darling, but you certainly wouldn't have been the first person to try.'

'I don't want to live here,' she yells. 'I don't want to be here!'

Despite herself, the tears start up again.

'I know, doll, I know,' Grandma Betty says. She pulls Liz into an embrace and begins to stroke Liz's hair.

'My mother strokes my hair that way,' Liz says as she pulls away. She knows Grandma Betty meant to be comforting, but it only felt creepy—like her mother was touching her from beyond the grave.

Grandma Betty sighs and opens the passenger-side door. 'I'll drive the rest of the way home,' she says. Her voice sounds tired and strained.

'Fine,' says Liz stiffly. A moment later, she adds in a softer voice, 'Just so you know, I don't usually drive this badly, and I'm not usually this, like, emotional.'

'Perfectly understandable,' Grandma Betty says. 'I had already assumed that might be the case.'

As she slides back over to the passenger seat, Liz suspects that it will be some time before Grandma Betty lets her drive again. But Liz doesn't know Grandma Betty and she is wrong. At that moment, Grandma Betty turns to her and says, 'If you want, I'll teach you three-point turns and parallel parking. I'm not sure, but I think you can still get your driver's license here.'

'Here?' Liz asks.

'Here in Elsewhere.' Grandma Betty pats Liz on the hand before starting the car. 'Just let me know.'

Liz appreciates what it must have taken Grandma Betty to even make this offer, but this isn't what she wants. For her, it's not about the three-point turns and the parallel parking. She wants to finish driver's ed. She wants a Massachusetts state driver's license. She wants to drive aimlessly with her friends on the weekends and discover mysterious new roads in Nashua and Watertown. She wants the ability to go anywhere without a grandmother or anyone else. But she knows this will never happen. For she is here, Elsewhere, and what good is a driver's license if the only place she can use it is here?

Waking

A taxicab speeds out of nowhere. Liz flies through the air. She thinks, I will surely die.

She wakes in a hospital room, her vision bleary, her head wrapped in bandages. Her mother and father stand at her bedside, dark circles under their eyes. 'Oh, Lizzie,' her mother says, 'we thought we'd lost you.'

Two weeks later, the doctor removes her bandages. Aside from a C-shaped arc of stitches over her left ear, she is as good as new. The doctor calls it the most remarkable recovery he has ever seen.

Liz returns to school. Everyone wants to hear about Liz's near-death experience. 'It's hard for me to talk about it,' she says. People think Liz has become *deep* since her accident, but the truth is, she just doesn't remember.

On her sixteenth birthday, Liz passes her driver's license test with flying colors. Her parents buy her a brand-new car. (They don't like her riding her bicycle anymore.) Liz applies to college. She writes her admissions essay on the time she was hit by a cab and how it changed her life. She is accepted early decision to her top choice, the Massachusetts Institute of Technology. Liz graduates MIT with a degree in biology, and then she attends veterinary school in Florida. One day, she meets a boy, the type of boy with whom she can imagine spending the rest of her life and maybe even—

'Rise and shine, Elizabeth!' Grandma Betty interrupts Liz's dream at seven the next morning.

Liz buries her head under the blankets. 'Go away,' she mutters, too low for Grandma Betty to hear.

Grandma Betty opens the curtains. 'It's going to be a beautiful day,' she says.

Liz yawns, her head still under the covers. 'I'm dead. What in the world do I have to get up for?'

'That's certainly a negative way of looking at things. There's loads to do in Elsewhere,' says Grandma Betty as she opens the next set of curtains. The room Liz is staying in (she can't think of it as *her* room; *her* room is back on Earth) has five windows. It reminds her of a greenhouse. What she really wants is a small dark room with few (preferably no) windows and black walls—something more appropriate to her current situation. Liz yawns as she watches Grandma Betty move onto the third window. 'You don't have to open all the curtains,' Liz says.

'Oh, I like a lot of light, don't you?' Grandma Betty replies.

Liz rolls her eyes. She can't believe she'll have to spend the rest of her life living with her grandmother, who is, make no mistake, an old person. Even though Grandma Betty looks like a young woman on the outside, Liz can tell she probably harbors all sorts of secret old-people tendencies.

Liz wonders what specifically Grandma Betty meant when she said there was "loads to do in Elsewhere." On Earth, Liz was constantly occupied with studying and finding a college and a career and all those other things that the adults in her life deemed terribly important. Since she had died, everything she was doing on Earth had seemed entirely meaningless. From Liz's point of view, the question of what her life would be was now definitively answered. The story of her life is short and pointless: There once was a girl who got hit by a car and died. The end.

'You have your acclimation appointment at eight thirty,' says Grandma Betty.

Liz removes her head from under the covers. 'What's that?'

'It's a sort of orientation for the newly dead,' says Grandma Betty.

'Can I wear this?' Liz indicates her white pajamas. She has been wearing them so long they are more precisely called gray pajamas. 'I didn't exactly have time to pack, you know.'

'You can borrow something of mine. I think we're about the same size, although you're probably a little smaller,' Grandma Betty says.

Liz considers Betty for a moment. Betty has larger breasts than Liz but is slim and about Liz's height. It is somehow strange to be the same size as her grandmother.

'Just pick something from my closet, and if you need anything shortened or taken in, let me know. I don't know if I mentioned that I'm a seamstress here,' Grandma Betty says.

Liz shakes her head.

'Yeah, keeps me pretty busy. People tend to get smaller as they get younger, so they always need their clothes taken in.'

'Can't they just buy new ones?' Liz asks, her brow furrowed.

'Of course, doll, I didn't mean to imply they couldn't. However, I have observed that there's less waste here, all around. And I do make new garments, too, you know. I prefer it, actually. It's more creative for me.'

Liz nods and feels relieved. The idea of everyone wearing the same clothes for the rest of time was one of the more depressing things she'd thought lately.

After a shower (which Liz finds gloriously equivalent to showers on Earth), she wraps a towel around herself and goes into Grandma Betty's closet.

The closet is large and well organized. Her grandmother's clothes look expensive and well made, but a bit theatrical for Liz's taste: felt cloches and old-fashioned dresses and velvet capes and brooches and ballet slippers and ostrich feathers and patent-leather high heels and fishnet stockings and fur. Liz wonders where her grandmother goes in these garments. She further wonders if Grandma Betty owns jeans, for the only thing Liz wants to wear is jeans and a T-shirt. She searches the closet for jeans. Aside from navy blue sailor pants, she finds nothing even close.

Completely frustrated, Liz sits down under a rack of sweaters. She imagines her messy closet back home with its twelve pairs of blue jeans. It had taken a long time to find all those jeans. She had had to try on many pairs. The thought of them makes Liz want to cry. She wonders what will happen to her jeans now. She puts her head in her hands and touches the stitches over her ear. Even getting dressed is difficult here, Liz thinks.

'Did you find anything?' Grandma Betty asks when she comes into the closet several minutes later. In this time, Liz has not moved.

Liz looks up but doesn't answer.

'I know how you feel,' Grandma Betty says.

Yeah right, Liz thinks.

'You're thinking that I don't know how you feel, but in some ways, I do. Dying at fifty isn't as different from dying at fifteen as you might think. When you're fifty, you still have a lot of things you might like to do and a lot of things you need to take care of.'

'What did you die from anyway?' Liz asks.

'Breast cancer. Your mother was pregnant with you at the time.'

'I know that part.'

Grandma Betty smiles a sad little smile. 'So, it's nice I get to meet you now. I was beside myself with disappointment that I didn't get to meet you then. I wish we'd met under slightly different circumstances, of course.' She shakes her head. 'You might look pretty in this.' She raises the arm of a floral print dress that is not at all like something Liz would wear.

Liz shakes her head.

'Or this?' Grandma Betty points to a cashmere sweater.

'If it's the same to you, I think I'll just wear my pajamas after all.'

'I understand, and you certainly won't be the first person to go to an acclimation appointment in pajamas,' Grandma Betty assures her.

'Your clothes are nice, though.'

'We can buy you some other things,' Grandma Betty says. 'I would have bought them for you myself, but I didn't know what you would like. Clothes are a personal business, at least for me.'

Liz shrugs.

'When you're ready,' Grandma Betty continues, 'I'll give you money. Just say the word.'

But Liz can't bring herself to care what she wears anymore and decides to change the subject. 'I've been wondering what I should call you, by the way. It seems odd to call you Grandma somehow.'

'How about Betty, then?'

Liz nods. 'Betty.'

'And what do you like to be called?' Betty asks.

'Well, Mom and Dad call me Lizzie . . .' Liz corrects herself. 'They used to call me Lizzie, but I think I prefer Liz now.'

Betty smiles. 'Liz.'

'I'm really not feeling well. Would it be all right if I stayed in bed today, and we changed my acclimation appointment to to-morrow?' asks Liz. Her collarbone feels tender where the seat belt pulled against it during last night's crash, but mainly Liz doesn't feel like doing anything.

Betty shakes her head. 'Sorry, doll, but everyone's got to have their acclimation appointment their first day in Elsewhere. No exceptions.'

Liz leaves the closet and turns to Betty's bedroom window, which overlooks an unruly garden. She can identify roses, lilies, lavender, sunflowers, chrysanthemums, begonias, gardenias, an apple tree, an orange tree, an olive tree, and a cherry tree. Liz wonders how so many varieties of flowers and fruits can share a single plot of land. 'Is that your garden?' Liz asks.

'Yes,' Betty answers.

'Mom likes to garden, too.'

Betty nods. 'Olivia and I used to garden together, but among other things, we never agreed about what to plant. She preferred useful plants like cabbages and carrots and peas. Me, I'm a sucker for a sweet perfume or a splash of color.'

'It's pretty,' Liz says, watching a monarch butterfly rest on a red hibiscus flower. 'Wild, but pretty.' The butterfly flaps its wings and flies away.

'Oh, I know I should probably trim everything back and impose some order on it, but I can never bring myself to prune a rosebush or clip a bud. A flower's life is short enough as it is.' Betty laughs. 'My garden is a beautiful mess, I'm afraid.'

'Are you sure you don't want to drive?' Betty asks on the way to Liz's meeting at the Registry.

Liz shakes her head.

'You shouldn't be discouraged just because you had a minor setback.'

'No,' Liz says firmly. 'If I'm getting younger anyway, I'm going to have to get used to being a passenger.'

Betty looks at Liz in the rearview mirror. In the backseat, Liz's arms are folded across the chest of her pajama shirt.

'I'm sorry about my tour guide routine last night,' Betty says.

'What do you mean?' Liz asks.

'I mean, I think I was trying too hard. I want you to like it here, and I want you to like me. But I think I just went on and on, and sounded like an idiot.'

Liz shakes her head. 'You were fine. I just . . .' Her voice trails off. 'I just don't really know you is all.'

'I know,' Betty says, 'but I know you a bit. I've watched you most of your life from the ODs.'

'What are ODs?'

'Observation Decks. They're these places where you can see all the way to Earth. For limited amounts of time, of course. Do you remember when you saw your funeral on the ship?'

'Yes,' says Liz, 'from the binoculars.' As long as she lived (died?), she would never forget it.

'Well, they have Observation Decks set up throughout Elsewhere. They'll go over it today at your acclimation appointment.'

Liz nods.

'Out of curiosity, is there anyone in particular you'd like to see?' Betty asks.

Of course, Liz misses her family. But in some ways the one person Liz misses the most is her best friend, Zooey. She wonders what Zooey's prom dress would look like. Would Zooey even go to prom now that Liz was dead? Zooey hadn't bothered to attend the funeral. If Zooey had been the one who died, Liz definitely would have gone to her funeral. Now that she thinks about it, it seems pretty rude that her own best friend had skipped out, particularly under the circumstances. After all, if Zooey hadn't asked Liz to the mall to look for dumb prom dresses, Liz wouldn't have been hit by a taxicab. If Liz hadn't been hit by a taxicab, she wouldn't have died, and . . . Liz sighs:

you could drive yourself crazy with ifs.

Suddenly, Betty gestures out the window, causing the car to swerve a little. 'That's where your appointment is. It's called the Registry. I pointed it out to you yesterday, but I don't know how much attention you were paying.'

Out her window, Liz sees a gargantuan, rather homely structure. The tallest building Liz has ever seen, it seems to stretch up to infinity. Despite its size, the Registry looks like a child built it: walls, stairways, and other additions jut out at improbable angles, and the construction seems improvised, almost like the makeshift forts Liz used to build with her brother. 'It's sort of ugly,' Liz pronounces.

'It used to be better looking,' says Betty, 'but the building's needs are always outpacing its size. Architects are constantly concocting ways to expand the building, and construction workers are constantly implementing those plans. Some people say the building looks like it's growing right before your eyes.'

Betty makes a left turn into the Registry parking lot. She stops the car in front of one of the building's multiple entrances. 'Do you want me to walk you inside? It can get kind of confusing in there,' Betty says.

'No, I'd rather go myself, if you don't mind,' Liz replies.

Betty nods. 'I'll pick you up around five, then. Try to have a good day, doll.'

A Circle and a Line

Although Liz has arrived at the Registry fifteen minutes early, it takes her nearly twenty-five minutes to find the Office of Acclimation. The maps posted at the elevator shaft are long outdated, and no one who works at the building seems able to give proper directions. When Liz attempts to retrace her footsteps, she keeps finding new doorways that she could swear weren't there five minutes earlier.

At random (for she now believes in the power of randomness as only the suddenly deceased can), Liz decides to give one of the new doorways a try. She finds a hallway and, at the end of the hallway, another door. An unofficial-looking cardboard sign indicates that behind this door lies the temporary home of the Office of Acclimation.

Liz opens the door. Inside, she finds a busy, perfectly ordinary-looking reception area. (As Betty had said, many people are still wearing white pajamas.) If not for a faded, rather macabre poster hanging on the wall, Liz might have thought she was at her doctor's office. The poster depicts a smiling gray-haired woman sitting up in a mahogany coffin. Printed on the poster are the following words:

SO YOU'RE DEAD, NOW WHAT?
The Office of Acclimation is here to help.

The peevish-looking woman at the front desk reminds Liz of the poster; she, too, is faded, dated, and grim. She wears her hair in a 1960s beehive and her skin has a greenish tint. A name-plate on her desk reads YETTA BROWN.

'Excuse me,' Liz says, 'I have an appointment at—'

Yetta Brown clears her throat and nods her head in the direction of a bell that sits on the desk. A sign by the bell reads, PLEASE RING FOR ASSISTANCE!!!

Liz obeys. Yetta Brown clears her throat again and plasters a broad fake smile across her face. 'Yes, how may I help you?'

'I have an appointment at eight—'

Yetta's fake smile turns into a definitive frown. 'Why didn't you say so? You're five minutes late for the video! Make haste, make haste, make haste!'

'I'm sorry,' Liz apologizes, 'I couldn't find—'

Yetta interrupts Liz again. 'I have no time for your apologies.'

Liz dislikes being interrupted. 'You shouldn't inter—'

'I have no time for small talk.'

Yetta deposits Liz in a dusty, darkened room with a battered VCR and TV. The room, which is more like a supply closet, barely has enough space for its one chair. 'I will return for you when the video is over,' Yetta says. 'Oh yes, enjoy the film,' she adds in a perfunctory manner as she walks out the door.

Liz sits in the lone chair. The video is like the dry informational videos that Liz occasionally watched for health in ninth grade or driver's ed in tenth grade on subjects like 'Sexual Education' and 'Traffic Safety.'

The video begins with a talking cartoon parrot. 'I'm Polly,' says the parrot. 'If you're watching this video, that means you're dead dead dead! Greetings and salutations, dead people!' Liz finds the animation primitive and Polly annoying.

With the detestable Polly as guide, the video covers some of what Liz and Betty have already discussed: how everyone in Elsewhere ages backward and becomes a baby, and how the babies are sent down the River when they are seven days old, back to Earth. 'On Earth,' Polly squawks, 'man ages from the time he is born to an indeterminate point in the future, when he will die die die.' The video shows a cartoon baby becoming a boy, then a man, then an old man, then dead. 'On Elsewhere,' Polly continues, 'a life is more finite: man dies, and ages backward until he is a baby.' The cartoon old man becomes a man, then a boy, then a baby. 'When man becomes a baby again, he is ready to be sent back to Earth, where the process begins again.' The cartoon baby becomes a boy, becomes a man, becomes an old man. Liz imagines her life depicted on a cartoon time line. I would only make it somewhere between cartoon boy and cartoon man, she thinks. And then she wonders if boys are always boys, and if girls are always girls, and if dogs are always dogs.

The video also ventures into subject matter that Liz and Betty had not discussed in much detail.

Liz learns the proper way to state her age: your current age followed by the number of years you have been in Elsewhere. Liz's current age is fifteen–zero. She also learns that her new "birthday" is January 4. It is a somewhat confusing calculation that involves adding the number of days past one's last birthday to the day one died.

She learns that no one new is born in Elsewhere, but no one dies either. People get sick and hurt, but with time, everyone eventually heals. Consequently, sickness isn't much of an issue here.

She learns that you are forbidden to make Contact with people on Earth ('Contact is a no-no! It's a no-no!' squawks Polly, waving his yellow beak furiously from side to side), but that you could view Earth from the Observation Decks anytime. Observation Decks, like the one on the SS *Nile*, aren't just for funerals. They are also located on docked boats and lighthouses scattered throughout Elsewhere. For the price of just one eternim, Liz could view whoever or whatever she wants back on Earth for five minutes. Liz decides right then to ask Betty to drive her to the nearest Observation Deck tonight.

She learns that everyone has to choose an avocation. From what Liz could tell, an avocation is basically like a job, except you are actually supposed to like doing it. Liz shakes her head at that part. How does she know what she wants to do? Not to mention, at her age, what is she even trained for?

She learns the official definition of *acclimation*. 'Acclimation,' yells Polly, 'is the process by which the newly deceased become residents of Elsewhere. So welcome welcome welcome, dead people!'

She learns many, many, many other things that she is sure she will probably forget.

The end of the video deals more with metaphysical issues on Elsewhere. It talks about how human existence is like a circle and a line at the same time. It is a circle, because everything that was old would be new and everything that was new became old. It is a line because the circle stretched out indefinitely, infinitely even. People die. People are born. People die again. Each birth and death is a little circle, and the sum of all those little circles is a life and a line. During this discussion of human existence, Liz finds herself drifting off to sleep.

She wakes several minutes later to the sound of Yetta Brown admonishing her. 'I hope you didn't sleep through the whole thing! Get up! Get up now!'

Liz jumps to her feet. 'I'm sorry. I'm just really exhausted from dying, and—'

Yetta Brown interrupts. 'It doesn't matter to me; your behavior only hurts yourself.' Yetta Brown sighs. 'You have your meeting with your acclimation counselor, Aldous Ghent, now. Mr. Ghent is a very important man. So, you know, it wouldn't do for you to fall asleep during your meeting with him.'

'I honestly don't think I missed much,' Liz apologizes.

'All right. Tell me why human existence is like a circle and a line,' Yetta demands.

Liz racks her brain. 'It's a circle because, um . . . Earth is a sphere, which is kind of like a, um, three-dimensional circle?'

Yetta shakes her head in disgust. 'Exactly as I thought!'

68

'Look, I'm sorry about falling asleep.' Liz speaks very quickly to avoid being interrupted. 'Maybe I can watch the end of the video again?'

Yetta Brown ignores Liz. 'We have a lot to get done today, Ms. Hall. Things will go far more smoothly if you can manage to stay awake.'

'This is Elizabeth Marie Hall, Mr. Ghent.' Yetta pronounces Liz's name as if it were a particularly unpleasant word like *gingivitis*. Aldous Ghent looks up as Yetta and Liz enter the office.

'Thank you, Ms. Brown,' Aldous calls as Yetta basically slams the door in his face. 'Ah well, perhaps she didn't hear me? Yetta seems to have peculiarly bad hearing. She's always interrupting me.'

Liz laughs politely.

'Hello, Elizabeth Hall. I am Aldous Ghent, your acclimation counselor. Please have a seat.' He indicates that Liz should sit in the chair in front of his desk. However, that chair is entirely covered in paperwork. Indeed, all of his windowless office is shrouded in paperwork.

'Should I move these files?' Liz asks.

'Oh, please do!' Aldous smiles and then looks sadly around his cluttered office. 'I have so much paperwork. I'm afraid my paperwork has paperwork.'

'Maybe you need a bigger office?' Liz suggests.

'They keep promising me one. It's the thing I'm most looking forward to. Except for my hair growing back.' He pats his bald pate affectionately. 'I started going bald around twenty-five, so I figure I only have around thirty-six more years to wait for a full head of hair. The sad part is, we all lose most of our hair when we become babies anyway. The way I see it, I'll only have about a twenty-four-year window of hair before I lose it all over again. Ah well!' Aldous sighs.

Liz runs her fingers through her own newly grown hair.

'Last year my teeth came back in. The teething was murder! I kept my wife up all night with my blubbering and ballyhoo.' Aldous grins so that Liz can see his teeth. 'I'm going to take good care of them this time around. Dentures are not good. They're worse than not good actually. Dentures, they um . . .'

'Suck?' Liz suggests.

'Dentures suck,' Aldous says with a laugh. 'They really do. The sound they make when you eat is just like sucking.'

Aldous carefully removes a file from the bottom of a precarious pile of paperwork in the center of his desk. He opens the file and reads aloud, 'You're from Bermuda where you died in a boating accident?'

'Um, that's not me,' Liz says.

'Sorry.' Aldous selects another file, 'You're from Manhattan, and had, uh, breast cancer, is it?'

Liz shakes her head. She doesn't even have much in the way of breasts.

Aldous selects a third file. 'Massachusetts? Head trauma in a bicycle accident?'

Liz nods. That's her.

'Well'—Aldous shrugs—'at least it was quick. Except for the coma part, but you probably don't remember that anyway.'

Indeed, Liz does not. 'How long was I in a coma?'

'About a week, but you were already brain-dead. Says here your poor parents had to decide to pull the plug. We, my wife Rowena and I, had to pull the plug on our son, Joseph, back on Earth. His best friend accidentally shot him when they were playing with an old gun of mine. It was the worst day of my life. If you ever have children—' Aldous stops himself.

'If I ever have children, what?'

'I'm sorry. I don't know why I said that. No one can have children on Elsewhere,' Aldous says.

Liz takes a moment to absorb this information. From Aldous's tone, she knows he thinks this news will upset her. But Liz hasn't really thought about having children.

'Do you see your son now?' Liz asks.

Aldous shakes his head. 'No, he was already back on Earth by the time Ro and I got here. I would have liked to see him again, but it was not to be.' Aldous blows his nose. 'Allergies,' he apologizes.

'What kind?' Liz asks.

'Oh,' Aldous replies, 'I'm allergic to sad memories. It's the worst. Would you like to see a picture of my wife, Rowena?'

Liz nods. Aldous holds out a silver frame with a picture of a lovely Japanese lady about Aldous's age. 'This is my Rowena,' he says proudly.

'She's very elegant,' Liz says.

'She is, isn't she? We died on the same day in a plane crash.'

'That's awful.'

'No,' Aldous says, 'we were actually very, very lucky.'

'For the longest time, I didn't even realize that I was dead,' Liz confides in Aldous. 'Is that normal?'

71

'Sure,' Aldous reassures her, 'people take all different amounts of time to acclimate. Some people reach Elsewhere, and they still think it's a dream. I knew a man who was here fifty years and went all the way back to Earth without catching on.' Aldous shrugs. 'Depends on how a person died, how old they were—it's lots of factors, and it's all part of the process. It can be particularly difficult for young people to realize they have passed,' Aldous says.

'Why is that?'

'Young people tend to think they're immortal. Many of them can't conceive of themselves as dead, Elizabeth.'

Aldous proceeds to go through all the things Liz would have to do in the next several months. Dying seems to entail a great deal more work than Liz initially thought. In a way, dying isn't that different from school.

'Do you have any initial thoughts about an avocation?' Aldous asks.

Liz shrugs. 'Not really. I didn't have a job on Earth because I was still in school.'

'Oh no, no, no,' Aldous says. 'An avocation is not a job. A job has to do with prestige! Money! An avocation is something a person does to make his or her soul complete.'

Liz rolls her eyes.

'I see by your expression you don't believe me,' Aldous says. 'It appears I've got a cynic on my hands.'

Liz shrugs. Who wouldn't be cynical in her situation?

'Is there anything you particularly loved on Earth?'

Liz shrugs again. On Earth, she was good at math, science, and swimming (she had even gotten her scuba certification last summer), but she didn't exactly *love* any of those activities.

'Anything, anything at all?'

'Animals. Maybe something with animals or dogs,' Liz says finally, thinking of her prized pug, Lucy, back on Earth.

'Marvelous!' crows Aldous. 'I'm sure I could find you something fabulous to do with dogs!'

'I'll have to think about it,' Liz says. 'It's a lot to take in.'

Aldous asks Liz a bit about her life on Earth. To Liz, her old life has already begun to seem like a story she is telling about someone else entirely. Once upon a time, a girl named Elizabeth lived in Medford, Massachusetts.

'Were you happy?' asks Aldous.

Liz thinks about Aldous's question. 'Why do you want to know?'

'Don't worry. It's not a test. It's just something I like to ask all my advisees.'

In truth, she hadn't put much thought into whether she was happy before. She supposes that since she never thought about it, she must have been happy. People who are happy don't really need to ask themselves if they are happy or not, do they? They just *are* happy, she thinks.

'I suppose I must have been happy,' Liz says. And as soon as she says it, she knows it's true. One silly little errant teardrop runs out of the corner of her eye. Liz quickly brushes it away. A second tear follows, and then a third, and it isn't long before she finds she is crying.

'Oh dear me, oh dear me!' exclaims Aldous. 'I'm sorry if my question upset you.' He excavates a box of tissues from underneath one of the towers of paperwork. He considers handing her one tissue and then decides on the entire box.

Liz looks at the tissue box, which is decorated with drawings of snowmen engaged in various holiday activities. One of the snowmen is happily placing a smiling rack of gingerbread men in an oven. Baking gingerbread men, or any cooking for that matter, is probably close to suicide for a snowman, Liz thinks. Why would a snowman voluntarily engage in an activity that would in all likelihood melt him? Can snowmen even eat? Liz glares at the box.

Aldous pulls out a tissue and holds it up to Liz's nose as if she were five years old. 'Blow,' he orders her.

Liz obeys. 'I seem to cry a lot lately.'

'Perfectly natural.'

Liz had been happy. How remarkable, she thinks. The whole time she had been on Earth she hadn't considered herself a particularly happy person. Like many people her age, she had been moody and miserable for what she now sees as totally foolish reasons: she had not been the most popular person in school, she didn't have a boyfriend, her brother could be annoying, and she had freckles. In many ways, she had felt that she had been waiting for all the good things to happen: living alone, going to college, driving a car. Now Liz finally sees the truth. She had been happy. Happy, happy, happy. Her parents had loved her; her best friend had been the most sympathetic, wonderful girl in the world; school had been easy; her brother hadn't been all that bad; her pug had liked to sleep next to her in bed; and, yes, she had even been considered pretty. Until a week ago, Liz realizes, her life had been entirely without obstacle. It had been a happy, simple existence, and now it was over.

'Are you all right?' Aldous asks, his voice filled with concern.

Liz nods, even though she does not feel all right. 'I miss my dog, Lucy.' She wonders whose bed Lucy is sharing now.

Aldous smiles. 'Luckily, dog lives are much shorter than human lives. You may get to see her again someday.'

Aldous clears his throat. 'I meant to mention this before. People who die as young as you, that is to say, sixteen and under, can be sent back to Earth early.'

'What do you mean?' asks Liz.

'Young people sometimes find the process of adjusting to life in Elsewhere quite difficult and their acclimations ultimately fail. So, if you choose, you can go back to Earth early. As long as you declare your intentions within your first year of residence. It's called the Sneaker Clause.'

'Would I go back to my old life?'

Aldous laughs. 'Oh no, no, no! You would start all over again as a baby. Of course, you might run into people you used to know, but they wouldn't know you, and in all likelihood, you wouldn't recognize them.'

'Is there any way I could go back to my old life?'

Aldous looks at Liz sternly. 'Now I must warn you, Elizabeth. There is no way you can or should go back to your old life. Your old life is over, and you can never go back. You may hear of a place called the Well–'

'What's the Well?' Liz interrupts him.

'It's strictly forbidden,' says Aldous. 'Now about the Sneaker Clause–'

'Why is it forbidden?'

Aldous shakes his head. 'It just is. Now, about the Sneaker

Clause—'

'I don't think that's for me,' Liz interrupts. As much as she misses Earth, she realizes that what she misses about Earth is all the people she knows there. Without them, going back seems pointless. Not to mention, she doesn't want to be a baby just yet.

Aldous nods. 'Of course, you still have a year to decide.'

'I understand.' Liz pauses. 'Um, Aldous, can I ask you one more question?'

'You want to know where God is in all of this, am I right?' Aldous asks.

Liz is genuinely surprised. Aldous had read her mind. 'How did you know I was going to ask that?'

'Let's just say I've been doing this awhile.' Aldous takes off his tortoiseshell glasses and cleans them on his pants. 'God's there in the same way He, She, or It was before to you. Nothing has changed.'

How could Aldous say that? Liz wonders. For her, everything is changed.

'I think you'll find,' Aldous continues, 'that dying is just another part of living, Elizabeth. In time, you may even come to see your death as a birth. Just think of it as *Elizabeth Hall: The Sequel.*' Aldous replaces his glasses and looks at his watch. 'Good lord!' Aldous exclaims. 'Would you look at the time? We have to get you over to the Department of Last Words, or Sarah's going to have my head.'

Last Words

At the Department of Last Words, Liz is met by an efficient woman who reminds Liz of a camp counselor. 'Hello, Ms. Hall,' the woman says. 'I'm Sarah Miles, and I just need to confirm what your last words were.'

'I'm not sure I remember. For the longest time, I didn't even know I was dead,' Liz apologizes.

'Oh, that's all right. It's just a formality really,' says Sarah. She consults a musty encyclopedia-sized book. 'Right, it says here your last words, or I should say last word, was "um." '

Liz waits for Sarah to finish speaking. In fact, she is quite interested to know what her last words were. Would they be profound? Sad? Pathetic? Heartrending? Illuminating? Angry? Horrified? After several moments of silence, Liz realizes Sarah is staring at her. 'So,' says Liz.

'So,' replies Sarah, 'was it "um"?'

'Was it um what?' Liz asks.

'I meant, was your last word "um"?'

'You're saying the last thing I ever said was "um"?'

'That's what it says in the book, and the book's never wrong.' Sarah pats the tome affectionately.

'God, I can't believe how crappy that is.' Liz shakes her head.

'Oh, it's not that bad.' Sarah smiles. 'I've definitely heard worse.'

'I just wish I'd said something more . . .'–Liz pauses–'Something more, um . . .' Her voice trails off.

'Right.' Sarah sympathizes for exactly three seconds. 'So, I just need you to sign off on this.'

'If you already know what I said, why do you need me to sign off on them?' Liz is still steaming that the last thing she would ever say on Earth was "um."

'I don't know. It's just how things are done here.'

Liz sighs. 'Where do I sign?'

As Liz is leaving, she reflects on her last words. If your last words are somehow meant to encapsulate your entire existence, Liz finds *um* strangely appropriate. *Um* means nothing. *Um* is what you say while you're thinking of what you'll really say. *Um* suggests someone interrupted before they'd begun. *Um* is a fifteen-year-old girl who gets hit by a taxicab in front of a mall on the way to help pick out a prom dress for a prom she isn't even going to, for God's sake. *Um*. Liz shakes her head, vowing to omit *um* and all equally meaningless words (*uh, like, huh, sorta, kinda, oh, hey, maybe*) from her vocabulary.

Back in the lobby of the Office of Acclimation, Liz is happy to spot a familiar face. 'Thandi!'

Thandi turns around, smiling broadly at Liz. 'You just do your last words, too?'

Liz nods. 'Apparently, all I said was "um," although I was too screwed up to remember anyway. How were yours?'

'Well'—Thandi hesitates—'I can't really repeat them.'

'Come on,' Liz prods, 'I just told you mine, and they were totally lame.'

'Oh, all right, if you really want to know. The gist was 'Jesus Christ, Slim, I think I've been shot in the head!' Only I said the f-word a couple times, too. And then I died.'

Liz laughs a little. 'At least you were descriptive and accurate.'

Thandi shakes her head. 'I wish I hadn't cursed, though. I wasn't raised that way, and now it's on my permanent record.'

'Cut yourself some slack, Thandi. I mean, you'd just been shot in the head. I think, under the circumstances, it's okay you said "fu—" '

Thandi interrupts her. 'Don't you go saying it now!'

At that moment, Aldous Ghent bounds into the lobby. 'Oh dear, I hope I'm not interrupting,' he says, 'but I need to speak to Elizabeth for a moment.'

'No,' says Thandi, 'I was just leaving.' She whispers to Liz, 'I'm really glad to see you. I was so worried you would stay on that boat forever.'

Liz just shakes her head and changes the subject. 'Where are you staying now?'

'I live with my cousin Shelly—I think I mentioned her before.'

'Is she'—Liz pauses—'better now?'

Thandi smiles. 'She is, and thanks for asking. You should

come visit. I told Shelly all about you. Come whenever. She's not much older than us, so she's cool with having people over.'

'I'll try,' Liz says.

'Well, I hope you'll do better than that,' says Thandi as she leaves.

'Pretty hair,' says Aldous, watching Thandi walk away.

'Yes,' Liz agrees.

'Well, Elizabeth, I've just had the most fantastic idea,' says Aldous. 'You mentioned before that you might like to work with animals?'

'Yes.'

'A position has just opened up, and as soon as I saw it, I thought of you.'

'Why, Aldous,' I said to myself, 'this is positively providential!'

'So will you do it?' Aldous stands there beaming at Liz.

'Um, what is it?' There was that word again.

'Oh yes, of course! Leave it to me to put the horse before the cart. Or rather, the cart before the horse. The horse is supposed to go before the cart, I believe. I have limited experience with both horses and carts. Oh yes, the position! The position's in the Division of Domestic Animals of the Department of Acclimation.'

'What's that?' asks Liz.

'It's kind of like what I do actually,' says Aldous Ghent, 'only it's with people's passed pets. I'm quite sure you'd be perfect for it.'

'Um,' Liz says. Why can't I stop saying *um*? she thinks. 'Um, it sounds interesting.'

'By the way, you do speak Canine, don't you?'

'Canine?' asks Liz. 'What's Canine?'

'Canine is the language of dogs. Dear me, you don't mean to say that they *still* aren't teaching it in Earth schools?' Aldous seems truly horrified at the possibility.

Liz shakes her head.

'A pity,' says Aldous, 'as Canine is one of our most beautiful languages. Did you know that there are over three hundred words for *love* in Canine?'

Liz thinks of her sweet Lucy back on Earth. 'I believe it,' Liz says.

'It has always seemed a weakness of an Earth education that children are only taught to communicate with their own species, don't you think?' asks Aldous.

'Since I don't speak, uh, Canine, does that mean I couldn't work at the Department of . . . What did you call it again?'

'Department of Acclimation, Division of Domestic Animals. And not necessarily. How fast do you pick up foreign languages, Elizabeth?'

'Pretty fast,' Liz lies. Spanish was her worst subject in school.

'Are you sure?' Aldous cocks his head thoughtfully at Liz.

'Yes, and if it matters, I even wanted to be a veterinarian when I was on Earth.'

'A marvelous profession, but unfortunately, or perhaps fortunately, we don't need those here. Time and rest are the only healers. One of the many benefits of living in a reverse-aging culture. Elsewhere doesn't have doctors, either. Although we do have nurses for animals and humans both, and of course our share of psychologists, therapists, psychiatrists, and other mental health professionals. Even when the body is well, you still find that the mind . . . Well, the mind has a mind of its own.' Aldous laughs. 'But I digress.'

'So, the position? It's perfect, right?' He beams at Liz.

At first, Liz thought the job sounded like something she might enjoy, but now she isn't so sure. What is the point of learning a whole new job (not to mention a whole new language) when she'd just be going back to Earth in fifteen years anyway? 'I'm just not sure,' Liz says finally.

'Not sure? But a moment ago, you seemed so–'

Liz interrupts. 'It sounds cool, but . . .' She clears her throat. 'I just think I need to take some time to myself first. I'm still sort of getting used to the idea of being dead.'

Aldous nods. 'Perfectly natural,' he says, and nods again. Liz can see his nods are meant to conceal his disappointment.

'I don't have to decide today, do I?' Liz asks.

'No,' Aldous says. 'No, you don't have to decide today. We'll talk again next week. Of course, the position may be filled by then.'

'I understand,' she says.

'I must caution you, Elizabeth. The longer you wait to start your new life, the harder it may become.'

'My new life? What new life?' Liz's voice is suddenly hard, her eyes cold.

'Why, this one,' says Aldous, 'this new life.'

Liz laughs. 'That's just words, isn't it? You can call it life, but it's really just death.'

'If this isn't life, then what is it?' Aldous asks.

'My life is on Earth. My life is not here,' Liz says. 'My life is with my parents and my friends. My life is over.'

'No, Elizabeth, you are completely, absolutely, totally wrong.'

'I'm dead,' she says. 'I'M DEAD!' she yells.

'Dead,' Aldous says, 'is little more than a state of mind. Many people on Earth spend their whole lives dead, but you're probably too young to understand what I mean.'

Yes, Liz thinks, exactly my point. She hears a clock strike five. 'I have to go. My grandmother's waiting for me.'

Watching Liz run off, Aldous calls after her, 'Promise you'll think about the position!'

Liz doesn't answer. She finds Betty's car parked in front of the Registry. Liz opens the door and gets in. Before Betty can say a single word, Liz asks, 'Would it be okay if we went to one of the Observation Decks?'

'Oh, Liz, it's your first real night here. Wouldn't you prefer to do something else? We can do whatever you want.'

'What I'd really like to do is see Mom and Dad and Alvy. And my best friend, Zooey. And some other people, too. Is that okay?'

Betty sighs. 'Are you sure, doll?'

'I really, really want to go.'

'All right,' Betty says finally, 'there's one near the house.'

Sightseeing

'd come with you,' Betty says. She stops her car on the narrow strip of road that runs parallel to the beach. 'I haven't seen Olivia in the longest time.'

'Mom's old now,' says Liz. 'She's older than you.'

'It's hard to believe. Where does the time go?' Betty sighs. 'I've always hated that phrase. It makes it sound like time went on holiday, and is expected back any day now. "Time flies" is another one I hate. Apparently, time does quite a bit of traveling, though.' Betty sighs again. 'So, do you want me to come with you?'

Liz would like nothing less than for Betty to accompany her. 'I might be a while,' Liz says.

'These places. They can be dangerous, doll.'

'Why?'

'People get obsessed. It's like a drug.'

Liz looks at the red lighthouse, which has a row of brightly lit glass windows at the top. The windows remind Liz of teeth. She can't decide if the lighthouse looks like it's smiling or snarling. 'How do I get inside?' Liz asks.

'Follow the path until you reach the entrance.' Betty points out the car window: a wooden boardwalk, gray with water and time, joins the red lighthouse tenuously to the land. 'Then take the elevator to the top floor. That's where you'll find the Observation Deck.'

Betty takes her wallet out of the glove compartment. She removes five eternims from her change purse and places them in Liz's hand. 'These will buy you twenty-five minutes of time. Is that enough?'

Liz thinks, I have no idea what enough time would be. How long does it take to say goodbye to everything and everyone you've ever known? Does it take twenty-five minutes, a little longer than a sitcom without the commercials? Who knows? 'Yes, thank you,' she says, closing her hand around the coins.

In the elevator, Liz stands next to a willowy blonde in a black shift dress. The woman sobs quietly, but in a way that is meant to attract attention.

'Are you all right?' Liz asks her.

'No, I most certainly am not.' The woman stares at Liz with bloodshot eyes.

'Did you die just recently?'

'I don't know,' the woman says, 'but I prefer to grieve alone, if you don't mind.'

Liz nods. She's sorry she even asked.

A moment later, the woman continues. 'I'm in mourning for

my life and I'm more unhappy than you can even imagine.' The woman puts on a pair of black cat-eye sunglasses. So adorned, she continues to weep for the remainder of the elevator ride.

This Observation Deck, or OD, looks almost exactly like the one on the SS *Nile* except it is smaller. The room has windows on all sides, lined with a tidy row of binoculars. Liz notes that not everyone who visits the OD is as unhappy as the weeping woman on the elevator.

A plump middle-aged woman with a bad perm sits in a glass box by the elevator. She waves the weeping woman through the turnstile that separates the OD from the elevator. The weeping woman nods curtly and checks her reflection in the attendant's glass box.

'That woman's in love with her own grief,' the attendant says, shaking her head. 'Some people just love all that drama.' She turns to Liz. 'You're new, so I'll give you my little spiel. Our hours are seven a.m. to ten p.m., Monday through Friday, ten a.m. to twelve a.m. Saturday, and seven a.m. to seven p.m. Sunday. We're open three hundred sixty-five days a year, including holidays. One eternim gets you five minutes of time, and you can buy as much time as you want. The price is not negotiable. Whether you want five minutes or five hundred minutes, the rate is the same. The operation of the binoculars should be like ones you've encountered before. Just press the side button for a different view, turn the eyepieces to adjust focus, and pivot the head as necessary. I'm Esther, by the way.'

'Liz.'

'You just get here, Liz?' Esther asks.

'How can you tell?'

'You have that shell-shocked, recently arrived look about you. Don't worry, honey. It'll pass, I promise. What'd you die of?'

'Hit by a car. And you?' Liz asks politely.

'Alzheimer's disease, but I guess it was the pneumonia that really did me in,' Esther answers.

'What was that like?'

'Can't say I remember,' Esther says with a laugh, 'and that's probably just as well.'

Liz selects Binoculars #15, which faces the land. After all the time on the *Nile*, Liz has grown tired of water. She sits on the hard metal stool and places an eternim in the slot.

Liz watches her family first. Her parents are sitting across from each other on opposite sides of the dining room table. Her mother looks like she's been awake for days. She smokes a cigarette, even though she'd quit when she became pregnant with Liz. Her father appears to be doing the *New York Times* crossword puzzle, but he isn't really. He just keeps tracing over the same answer (CHAUVINISM) with his pencil until he's pierced the newspaper all the way through and is writing on the tablecloth. In the living room, Alvy watches cartoons, even though it's a school night and her parents don't allow Liz and her brother to watch television on school nights, no exceptions. The phone rings. Liz's mother jumps to answer it. At that moment, the binoculars' lenses click closed.

By the time Liz puts a second eternim in the slot, her mother is off the phone. Alvy enters the dining room, wearing a ceramic flowerpot on his head. 'I'm a pothead!' he announces proudly.

'Take that off!' her mother screams at Alvy. 'Arthur, make your son behave!'

'Alvy, take the pot off your head,' Liz's father says in a measured voice.

'But I'm a pothead!' Alvy persists, even though his joke is not at all playing.

'Alvy, I'm warning you.' Liz's father is serious now.

'Oh, all right.' Alvy removes the pot and leaves the room.

Thirty seconds later, Alvy is back. This time he carries an old wicker Easter basket in his mouth.

'Urmph uf raket ash,' says Alvy.

'Now what?' Liz's mother asks.

'Urmph uf rasket ace,' Alvy repeats with improved enunciation.

'Alvy, take the basket out of your mouth,' Liz's father says. 'No one can understand you.'

Alvy obeys. 'I'm a basket case, get it?'

Alvy is met with blank stares.

'I'm carrying a basket in my mouth, so I'm a basket case—'

Liz's father takes the basket with one hand and tousles Alvy's hair with the other. 'We all miss Lizzie, but that's really no way to honor your sister.'

'Why?' Alvy asks.

'Well, prop comedy has traditionally been viewed as the lowest form of humor, son,' Liz's father says in his teaching voice.

'But I'm a basket case,' Alvy says plaintively. 'Like Mom,' he adds.

The lenses click shut before Liz gets to see her mother's reaction. With her next coin, Liz decides to watch someone else.

She settles on Zooey.

Zooey is sitting on her bed, talking on the phone. Her eyes are red from crying. 'I just can't believe she's gone,' Zooey says.

Now this is more like it, Liz thinks. At least someone knows how to mourn properly. Liz can't hear the other side of the conversation but feels sufficiently gratified by Zooey's grief to continue listening.

'I broke up with John. I mean, if he hadn't asked me to the prom, I wouldn't have told Liz to meet me at the mall, and she wouldn't be . . .' Her voice trails off.

'No!' Zooey says adamantly. 'I do not want to go!' And then, a moment later in a softer voice, 'Besides, I don't even have a dress . . .' Zooey twirls the phone cord around her ankle with her foot. 'Well, there was this black strapless one . . .' The lenses click shut.

Her last two eternims later, Liz is still not sure whether Zooey will or will not go to prom. During that time, Zooey does cry twice. Her tears make Liz happy. (Liz is only a little ashamed that her best friend's tears make her happy.)

At first, Liz feels bad about listening in on her loved ones, but the feeling doesn't last long. She rationalizes that she is really doing this for them. Liz imagines herself as a beautiful, benevolent, generous angel looking down on everyone from . . . from wherever she is.

Leaving the lighthouse that night, Liz realizes that it will take many more eternims to follow the goings on of all her friends and family. (She spent three whole eternims on that small portion of Zooey's phone conversation alone.) If she isn't going to get totally behind, she calculates that she will probably need at least twenty-four eternims a day, or two hours, which amounts to five minutes for every one hour of real life.

'I'm going to need some eternims,' Liz announces to Betty during the short drive back to Betty's house, 'and I was hoping you would lend them to me.'

'Of course. What do you need them for?' Betty replies.

'Well,' says Liz, 'I want to spend some time at the ODs.'

'Liz, do you really think that's a good idea?' Betty looks at Liz with concern, which Liz finds annoying. 'Maybe it would be a better use of your time to think about an avocation?'

Liz has prepared herself for Betty's response and is ready with a convincing counterargument. 'The thing is, Betty, since I died so abruptly, I think it would help if I could, like, *make peace* with the people on Earth. I promise, it won't be forever.' Liz feels corny saying "make peace," but she knows adults respond to that sort of thing.

Betty nods. And then she nods some more. The nodding seems to help Betty weigh what Liz said. 'Whatever time you need, you should take,' Betty says finally. In addition, Betty agrees, as Liz knew she would, to provide Liz with the money.

Properly funded with twenty-four eternims a day, Liz establishes a routine. The OD is close enough to Betty's house that Liz can walk there. She arrives every morning when it opens and stays every night until it closes.

Liz continues wearing the pajamas she wore on the SS *Nile*. She still hates them, but she doesn't want anything new. She sleeps in the pajamas as well, removing them only twice a week for Betty to wash.

Liz usually spreads out her two hours of OD time over the whole day, but sometimes she splurges and uses a couple eternims at a time. If something particularly interesting is happening, Liz spends all her eternims at once.

A typical day follows: fifteen minutes watching her parents and her brother in the morning (three eternims), forty-five minutes at school with her friends and her classes (nine eternims), a half hour with Zooey after school (six eternims), and the remaining half hour (six eternims) at her discretion.

Liz particularly likes when someone mentions her at school. At first, her classmates seem to speak of her quite frequently, but as time progresses (and not much time at that), the mentions become fewer and fewer. Only Edward, Liz's ex-boyfriend, and Zooey still speak of her with any regularity. Zooey and Edward weren't friends when Liz was alive; Zooey had even encouraged Liz to end the relationship. Liz feels gratified by the pair's sudden closeness.

Liz knows her family still thinks about her, but they rarely speak of her. She wishes they would talk about her more often. Her mother regularly sleeps in Liz's bed. Sometimes she wears Liz's clothes, too, even though they are tight on her. Liz's father, an anthropology professor at Tufts University, takes a leave of absence from the college. He starts watching talk shows all day and all night. He justifies his rampant talk-show watching by telling Liz's mother he is researching a book about why people like talk shows. Despite ample evidence that no one is amused, Alvy continues trying to entertain the family with his unique brand of rebus-style prop humor. Liz watches him enact "coming out of the closet," "shooting fish in a barrel," and "watching time stand still." She particularly enjoys the "melon-head" routine, a variation on the original "pothead" one, which involves a gutted cantaloupe and Alvy without pants.

Once, Liz watches her parents having sex, which she finds both disgusting and fascinating. Her mother cries at the end. Her father turns on the television to catch the last half hour of *Montel*. The whole routine costs Liz less than one eternim.

Watching her parents, Liz thinks that she'll probably never have sex now. She'll probably spend the next fifteen years alone.

In between watching five-minute segments of the old world, Liz sometimes plays with the stitches over her ear. She can't bring herself to ask Betty where to go to have the stitches removed. She likes knowing they're there.

Liz is at the OD so often, she becomes familiar with the regulars.

There are the old ladies who knit, taking a casual peek in the binoculars every hour or so.

There are the frantic young mothers with their seemingly end-less supplies of coins. The mothers remind Liz of slot-machine players she had once seen on a summer vacation to Atlantic City.

There are the businessmen who shout directions at the binoculars as if anyone back on Earth could hear them anyway. Liz is reminded of her father watching a football game and the silly way he would yell at the television.

There is a young man (still older than Liz) who comes once a week, on Thursday nights. Even though he comes at night, he always wears dark sunglasses. And he always sits at the same pair of binoculars, #17. He carries a leather pouch with precisely twelve eternims in it. On each visit the man stays one hour, no longer, and then leaves.

One night Liz decides to talk to him. 'Who are you here to see?' she asks.

'Excuse me?' The young man turns around, startled.

'I see you here every week and I just wondered who you were here to see,' Liz says.

The man nods. 'My wife,' he says after a moment.

'Aren't you too young to have a wife?' she asks.

'I wasn't always this young.' He smiles sadly.

'Lucky you,' she says, as she watches the man walk away. 'See you next Thursday,' she whispers too softly for him to hear.

As Liz is now spending all day, every day, at the OD, she becomes aware of just how uncomfortable the binoculars' metal stools are. On her way out one evening, she asks the attendant, Esther, about them.

'Well, Liz,' Esther tells her, 'when chairs are uncomfortable, it's usually a sign you've been sitting in them too long.'

Time passes slowly and quickly. The individual hours, minutes, and seconds seem to drag on, yet nearly a month has passed. In this time, Liz has become an expert at refilling the slots for minimal interruption between five-minute segments. She has deep-set circles underneath her eyes from keeping her face pressed up against the binoculars.

Occasionally, Betty asks Liz if she's put any thought into an avocation.

'I'm still taking some time,' Liz always answers.

Betty sighs. She doesn't want to press. 'Thandiwe Washington called for you again. And Aldous Ghent.'

'Thanks. I'll try to call them back later this week,' Liz lies.

That night, Liz sees Betty kneeling by the side of the bed. Betty is praying to Liz's mother. 'Olivia,' she whispers, 'I don't want to burden you, as I suspect your life is probably difficult enough right now. I don't know how to help Elizabeth. Please send me a sign telling me what to do.'

'Elizabeth, we are going out today,' Betty announces the next morning.

'I've got plans,' Liz protests.

'What plans?'

'OD,' Liz mumbles.

'You can do that tomorrow. Today, we're going sightseeing.'

'But, Betty—'

'No buts. You've been here four whole weeks and you haven't seen a thing.'

'I've seen things,' Liz says.

'Yeah? Like what? And things back on Earth don't count.'

'Why not?' Liz demands.

'They just don't.' Betty is firm.

'I don't want to go sightseeing,' Liz says.

'Tough luck,' Betty replies. 'I'm not giving you money for the OD today, so you don't have any choice.'

Liz sighs.

'And if it isn't too much to ask, could you possibly wear something other than those dirty old pajamas?' Betty asks.

'Nope,' Liz replies.

'I'll lend you something, or if you don't want that, we can buy you something on the—'

Liz interrupts her. 'Nope.'

Outside, Betty rolls down the convertible top. 'Do you want to drive?' she asks.

'No.' Liz opens the passenger door and sits.

'Fine,' Betty says as she fastens her seat belt. But a moment later she demands, 'Well, why not? You should want to drive.'

Liz shrugs. 'I just don't.'

'I'm not mad about that first night, if that's what you think,' Betty says.

'Listen, Betty, I don't want to drive because I don't want to drive. There's no secret meaning here. Furthermore, if the whole point of this trip is sightseeing, I wouldn't exactly be able to sightsee while I was concentrating on my driving, now would I?'

'No, I suppose not,' Betty concedes. 'Aren't you going to wear your seat belt?'

'What's the point?' Liz asks.

'The same as on Earth: to keep you from crashing into the dashboard.'

Liz rolls her eyes but does fasten her seat belt.

'I thought we'd go to the beach,' Betty says. 'How does that strike you?'

'Whatever,' Liz says.

'Elsewhere has marvelous beaches, you know.'

'Fantastic. Wake me when we get there.' To avoid further conversation, Liz closes her left eye and pretends to sleep. With her right eye, she watches the sights of Elsewhere out her window.

Liz thinks how much it looks like Earth, and the resemblance makes her catch her breath. But there are differences, and those differences, as they tend to be, are in the details. Out her window, she spots a drive-in movie theater—she has never seen one before except in vintage photographs. On the highway, a girl of about six or seven wears a business suit and drives an SUV. In the distance, she sees the Eiffel Tower and the Statue of Liberty, both rendered as topiaries. Along the side of the road, Liz sees a series of small wooden signs, spaced about ten meters apart. There is a single line of verse printed on each sign:

YOU MAY BE DEAD,
BUT YOUR BEARD GROWS ON,
LADIES HATE STUBBLE,
EVEN IN THE BEYOND.
BURMA SHAVE

'What's Burma Shave?' Liz asks Betty.

'A kind of shaving cream. When I was alive, they used to have those wooden signs on all the highways in America,' Betty answers. 'Most of them were replaced by billboards by the time you were born, but they were quite popular for a time, as much as a sign can be popular.' Betty laughs. 'You'll find that Elsewhere is a place where many old fads go to die, too.'

'Oh.'

'I thought you were asleep,' Betty says, looking over at Liz.

'I am,' Liz replies. She recloses her left eye.

Liz notices that it's quieter here than on Earth. And she can see that, in its own way, Elsewhere is beautiful. Even though there's no design to it, the effect is lovely. And even though it's lovely, Liz still hates it.

About an hour later, Betty wakes Liz, who has fallen asleep for real. 'We're here,' Betty says.

Liz opens her eyes and looks out the window. 'Yup, looks like a beach,' she says. 'Just like the one right by the house.'

'The point is the journey,' Betty says. 'Don't you want to get out of the car?'

'Not really, no,' Liz replies.

'Let's at least go in the gift shop and stretch our legs a bit,' Betty pleads. 'Maybe you'd like to get a souvenir?'

Liz looks doubtfully at the hut with the thatched roof near the water's edge. Given its location and construction, the shop looks like it could blow away at any moment. An incongruously sturdy metal sign hangs over the porch:

WISH YOU WERE HERE
KNICKKNACKS, BRIC-A-BRAC, BIBELOTS,
TRINKETS, GEWGAWS, NOVELTIES, WHIMSIES, WHATNOTS,
AND OTHER SUNDRIES FOR THE DISCRIMINATING BUYER

'So, what do you say?' Betty smiles at Liz.

'And who would I be buying a souvenir for exactly?' Liz asks.

'For yourself.'

'You buy souvenirs to take back to other people,' Liz snorts. 'I don't know anyone else and I'm not going back.'

'Not always, not yet,' Betty replies. 'Come on, I'll buy you whatever you want.'

'I don't want anything,' Liz says as she follows Betty into the tacky gift shop. No one is inside. A soup can sits by the cash register with a note: 'Out to lunch. Leave payment in can. Cut yourself a good deal, just between us.'

To satisfy Betty, Liz selects a book of six Elsewhere post-cards and a plastic snow globe. The snow globe has a minia-ture SS *Nile* submerged in sickly blue water. WISH YOU WERE HERE is written in red across the base of the dome.

'Do you want an Elsewhere beach towel?' Betty asks as Liz sets her two items on the counter.

'No, thank you,' Liz replies.

'Are you sure?'

'Yes,' Liz says tightly.

'Maybe a T-shirt, then?'

'No,' Liz yells. 'I don't want a goddamn T-shirt! Or a beach towel! Or anything else! All I want is to go home!'

'All right, doll,' Betty says with a sigh. 'I'll meet you outside. I just have to add everything up.'

Liz storms out of the store, carrying her new snow globe. She waits for Betty in the car.

Liz shakes the snow globe. The tiny SS *Nile* thrashes wildly in its plastic dome. Liz shakes the snow globe even harder. Slimy, stale blue water leaks onto Liz's hand. There's a small gap where the two seams of the dome were fused together. Liz opens the car door and throws the snow globe onto the pave-ment. Instead of shattering or cracking, it bounces across the parking lot like a rubber ball, stopping at the feet of a small girl in a pink polka-dotted bikini.

'You dropped this,' the girl calls out to Liz.

'Yes,' Liz agrees.

'Don't you want it?' The girl picks up the snow globe from the ground.

Liz shakes her head.

'Can I have it?' the girl asks.

'Knock yourself out,' Liz replies.

'The sky don't fall here, not much,' the girl says. She flips the globe over so that all the snow collects in the dome. She places her pinky over the leak.

'What do you mean?' Liz asks.

'Like this.' The girl flips the snow globe over.

'You mean snow,' Liz says. 'You mean it doesn't snow here.'

'Not much, not much, not much,' she sings. The girl walks over to Liz. 'You're big.'

Liz shrugs.

'How many are you?' the girl asks.

'Fifteen.'

'I'm four,' the girl answers.

Liz looks at the child. 'Are you a real little girl or a fake little girl?'

The girl opens her eyes as wide as they'll go. 'What do you mean?'

'Are you really four, or are you just pretend four?' Liz asks.

'What do you *mean*?' The girl raises her voice.

'Were you always four or did you used to be big?'

'I don't know. I'm four. Four!' the girl cries. 'You're mean.' The girl drops the snow globe at Liz's feet and runs away.

Liz picks it up and gives it another shake. She drains it of all the remaining blue liquid until the only thing left is a cluster of fake snow crystals.

Betty emerges from the gift shop, carrying a small paper bag.

'I bought this for you,' Betty says to Liz. She tosses Liz the paper bag. Inside is a T-shirt with the slogan MY GRANDMOTHER WENT TO ELSEWHERE AND ALL SHE GOT ME WAS THIS STINKY T-SHIRT.

For the first time that day, Liz smiles. 'It does stink,' Liz agrees. She puts the T-shirt on over her pajamas.

'I thought you'd like it,' Betty says. 'I said to myself, there aren't going to be too many opportunities where that T-shirt actually makes sense as a gift.' Betty laughs.

For the first time, Liz really looks at Betty. She has dark brown hair and light laugh lines around the eyes. Betty is pretty, Liz thinks. Betty looks like Mom. Betty looks like me. Betty has a sense of humor . . . Suddenly Liz realizes that her grandmother may have better things to do than worry about a surly teenager. She wants to apologize for today and for everything else. She wants to say she knows that none of this situation is Betty's fault. 'Betty,' she says softly.

'Yes, doll, what is it?'

'I . . . I'm . . .' Liz begins. 'My snow globe has a leak.'

That night, Liz writes out all six of the Elsewhere postcards. She writes one to her parents, one to Zooey, one to Edward, one to Lucy, one to Alvy. The last one she writes is to her biology teacher, who had skipped her funeral.

Dear Dr. Fujiyama,

By now, you have probably heard that I'm dead. This means I won't be attending this year's regional science fair, which is a great disappointment to me as I'm sure it also is for you. At the time I died, I felt I was starting to make real progress with those earthworms.

I really enjoyed your class and continue to follow along from the place where ~~I'm now living~~ I now find myself. Dissecting the pig looked pretty interesting, and I thought I might try it. Unfortunately, there aren't any dead pigs here for me to dissect.

It isn't bad here. The weather is nice most of the time. I live with my grandmother Betty now who is old, but looks young. (Long story.)

I was disappointed not to see you at the funeral as you were my favorite teacher even including middle and elementary school. Not to give you a hard time or anything, Dr. F :)

Yours,

Elizabeth Marie Hall, 5th Period Biology

Liz puts postage on all six postcards. She places them in the mail, knowing full well that they will never arrive at their intended destination. Lacking a return address, at least the postcards won't come back to her either. Liz thinks it might be nice to write a postcard to someone who would actually have a chance of receiving it.

Back at the ODs, Liz is starting to be frustrated with viewing her life in five-minute chunks. As soon as she gets involved in watching one story, the binoculars click closed. She feels like she is always missing something. For example, the prom is coming up. Zooey recently decided she would go with John after all. And, as long as Zooey is going, Liz would really prefer to see the whole thing, uninterrupted. Maybe if she had forty-eight eternims instead of twenty-four, she could keep up better? She decides to ask Betty for more eternims.

'Betty, I could use a couple more eternims each day.'

'How many did you have in mind?' Betty asks.

'I was thinking, maybe forty-eight a day.'

'That's starting to be a lot, doll.'

'I'll pay you back eventually,' Liz promises.

'It's not the eternims. I just worry about you spending so much time at the Observation Decks.'

'You're not my mother, you know.'

'I know, Liz, but I still worry.'

'God, I hate this!' Liz storms out of the room and throws herself on her bed. As she lies there, she decides to skip the ODs for three days in order to save up the eternims for the prom. This is a great sacrifice. Lacking friends or any other diversions, she spends the time in her room at Betty's house, worrying that she is falling behind with everyone back home. The three days seem endless, but she saves enough money to see the whole prom.

Liz also convinces Esther to let her stay after closing. Esther doesn't exactly agree, but she makes a point of showing Liz where the light switches are.

On prom night Liz watches Zooey eat strawberries dipped in chocolate, make photo key chains, and slow-dance to a schmaltzy ballad. Not long after, she sees Zooey lose her virginity in a fancy room at the same hotel where the dance was held. Out of respect for Zooey, Liz only watches for thirty seconds and covers her right eye with her hand. Liz pays special attention to Zooey's prom dress. The dress, the one Liz was meant to have helped her choose, is balled up in a corner of the room.

Liz leaves before her time runs out, two whole hours before the OD is even set to close. She doesn't want to face Betty at home, but she has nowhere else to go. Liz decides to sit in the park near Betty's house.

After a while, a white, fluffy bichon frise sits next to Liz on the bench. 'Hello,' the dog seems to say.

By way of greeting, Liz pats the dog on the head. It is the way it was with Lucy somehow, and Liz is even more homesick than she was before.

The dog cocks its head. 'You seem a little blue.'

'Maybe a little.'

'What's bothering you?' the dog asks.

Liz thinks about the dog's question before she answers. 'I'm lonely. Also, I hate it here.'

The dog nods. 'Would you mind scratching under my collar on the back of my neck? I can't reach there with my paws.'

Liz obliges.

'Thank you. That feels much better.' The dog snorts with pleasure. 'So, you said you were lonely and you hate it here?'

Liz nods again.

'My advice to you is to stop being lonely and to stop hating it here. That always works for me,' says the dog. 'Oh, and be happy! It's easier to be happy than to be sad. Being sad takes a lot of work. It's exhausting!'

A woman calls the dog from across the park: 'ARNOLD!'

'Gotta go! That's my two-legger calling me!' The dog hops off the bench. 'See you around!'

'See you,' says Liz, but the dog is already gone.

Lucky Cab

Following the prom, Liz gives up watching Zooey or anyone else from school. Now she watches only her immediate family.

One night just as the OD is about to close, Liz asks Esther, 'How do the binoculars even work?'

Esther makes a face. 'You should know that by now. You put in your coin and then—'

Liz interrupts. 'I meant, how do they *really* work? I spend pretty much every waking hour here and I don't know a thing about them.'

'Like any binoculars, I suppose. A series of convex lenses in two cylindrical tubes combine to form one image—'

Liz interrupts again. 'Yes, I know that part. I learned all that in, like, fifth grade.'

'Seems like you know everything, Liz, so I don't see why

you're bothering me.'

Liz ignores Esther. 'But Earth is so far, and these binoculars don't even seem particularly powerful. How could you possibly see all the way back to Earth?'

'Maybe that's the thing. Maybe Earth's not far at all.'

Liz snorts. 'That's a pretty thought, Esther.'

'It is, isn't it?' Esther smiles. 'I think of it like a tree, because every tree is really two trees. There's the tree with the branches that everyone sees, and then there's the upside-down root tree, growing the opposite way. So Earth is the branches, growing up to the sky, and Elsewhere is the roots, growing down in opposing but perfect symmetry. The branches don't think much about the roots, and maybe the roots don't think much about the branches, but all the time, they're connected by the trunk, you know? Even though it seems far from the roots to the branches, it isn't. You're always connected, you just don't think about—'

'Esther!' Liz interrupts a third time. 'But how do the binoculars work? How do they know what I want to see?'

'It's a secret,' Esther replies. 'I could tell you, but I'd have to kill you.'

'That isn't at all funny.' Liz starts to walk away.

'All right, Lizzie, I'll tell you. Come really close, and I'll whisper it in your ear.'

Liz obeys.

'Ask me again,' Esther says, 'and say please.'

'Esther, how do the binoculars work, please?'

Esther leans in toward Liz's ear and whispers, 'It's'—she pauses—'magic.' Esther laughs.

'I don't know why I even bother talking to you.'

'You don't have any friends and you're profoundly lonely.'

'Thanks.' Liz storms out of the OD.

'See you tomorrow, Liz,' Esther calls cheerily.

August 12, the day that would have been Liz's sixteenth birthday on Earth, arrives. Like every other day, Liz spends this one at the ODs.

'Lizzie would have been sixteen today,' her mother says to her father.

'I know,' he says.

'Do you think they'll ever find the man who did it?'

'I don't know,' he answers. 'I hope so,' he adds.

'It was a cab!' Liz yells at the binoculars. 'AN OLD YELLOW TAXICAB WITH A FOUR-LEAF-CLOVER AIR FRESHENER HANGING FROM THE REARVIEW MIRROR!'

'They can't hear you,' a grandmotherly type tells Liz.

'I know that,' Liz snaps. 'Shush!'

'Why didn't he stop?' Liz's mother asks her father.

'I don't know. At least he called 911 from the pay phone, not that it mattered anyway.'

'He still should have stopped.' Liz's mother starts to cry. 'I mean, you hit a fifteen-year-old kid, you stop, right? That's what a decent person does, right?'

'I don't know, Olivia. I used to think so,' Liz's father says.

'And I refuse to believe no one saw anything! I mean some-one must have seen; someone must know; someone must—'

Liz's time runs out, and the lenses click shut. She doesn't move. She just stares into the closed lenses and lets her mind go black.

Liz is furious to learn that she was the victim of a hit-and-run. Whoever hit me should pay, she thinks. Whoever hit me should go to prison for a very long time, she thinks. At that moment, Liz resolves to find the cabbie and then to somehow find a way to tell her parents. She pops an eternim in the slot and begins to scour the Greater Boston area for old yellow taxicabs with four-leaf-clover air fresheners hanging from their rearview mirrors.

Liz systematically searches for the lucky cab (her name for it) by watching the parking lots and the dispatchers of all the cab companies that service the area near the Cambridgeside Galleria. Although there are only four cab companies that drive this area, it still takes her an entire week—and over five hundred eternims—to locate the lucky cab. Liz raises the additional eternims by asking Betty for clothes money. Betty is happy to oblige her and doesn't ask too many questions. She just crosses her fingers and hopes Liz is coming out of her funk.

The cabbie's license says his name is Amadou Bonamy. He drives cab number 512 for the Three Aces Cab Company. She recognizes the cab immediately. It has the four-leaf-clover air freshener and it is older than Alvy, maybe older than Liz, too. Looking at the car, Liz is surprised that it even withstood the impact of her body.

The day after Liz locates the cab, she watches its driver. Amadou Bonamy is tall with black curly hair. His skin is the color of a coconut shell. His wife is pregnant. He takes classes at Boston University at night. He always helps people with their luggage when he drives them to the airport. He never purposely takes the long route, even when the people he's driving are from out of town. He doesn't speed much, Liz notes. He seems to obey traffic laws religiously, Liz further notes. Despite his car's dilapidated condition, he takes good care of it, vacuuming the seats each day. He tells dumb jokes to his passengers. He listens to National Public Radio. He buys bread at the same place Liz's mother buys bread. He has a son at the same school as Liz's brother. He—

Liz pushes the binoculars away. She realizes she doesn't want to know this much about Amadou Bonamy. Amadou Bonamy is a murderer. He is my murderer, she thinks. He needs to pay. Like her mother had said, it isn't right to hit people with dirty old cabs, and then leave them to die in the street. Liz's pulse races. She needs to find a way to tell her parents about Amadou Bonamy. She stands up and walks out of the Observation Deck, feeling flush with purpose and more alive than she has felt in some time.

On her way out of the building, Liz passes Esther.

'Glad to see you leaving while it's still daylight out for once,' Esther says.

'Yeah.' Liz stops. 'Esther,' she says, 'you wouldn't know how to make Contact with the living, would you?'

'Contact?' says Esther. 'Why in the world do you want to know about that? Contact's for damned fools. Nothing good's ever come out of talking to the living. Nothing but hurt and bother. And goodness knows, we've all got enough of that already.'

Liz sighs. Given Esther's response, Liz knows she can't ask just anyone about Contact. Not Betty, who is worried enough about Liz already. Or Thandi, who is probably angry at her for not returning her calls. Or Aldous Ghent, who would never in a million years help Liz make Contact. Only one person might help her, and that was Curtis Jest. Unfortunately, Liz hadn't seen him since the day of their funerals back on the *Nile*.

Early on, several news stories had run on Elsewhere about Curtis's death. Because Curtis was a rock star and celebrity, people were interested in his arrival. The funny thing was, most of the people on Elsewhere hadn't even heard his music. Curtis was popular among people of Liz's generation, and there were relatively few people from Liz's generation on Elsewhere. So interest declined quickly. By Liz's birthday, Curtis Jest had faded into total obscurity.

Liz decides to brave calling Thandi, who now works at a television station as an announcer. She reads the names of upcoming arrivals to Elsewhere so that people know to go to the Elsewhere pier to greet them. Liz thinks Thandi might have news of Curtis Jest's whereabouts.

'Why do you want to talk to him?' Thandi asks. Her voice is hostile.

'He happens to be a very interesting person,' Liz says.

'They say he became a fisherman,' Thandi says. 'You'll probably find him down at the docks.'

A fisherman? she thinks. Fishing seems so ordinary. It doesn't make any sense. 'Why would Curtis Jest be a fisherman?' Liz asks.

'Beats me. Maybe he likes to fish?' Thandi suggests.

'But there are musicians on Elsewhere. Why wouldn't Curtis want to be a musician?'

Thandi sighs. 'He already did that once, Liz. And it obviously didn't make him very happy.'

Liz remembers those long marks and bruises on his arms. She isn't sure she will ever forget them. Still, it seems entirely wrong for Curtis to be anything other than a musician. Maybe she will ask him about that when she goes to see him.

'Thanks for the information,' Liz says.

'You're welcome,' Thandi replies. 'But you know, Elizabeth, it isn't right that you don't return a person's call for months and months, and when you finally get it in your head to call, you're only asking about someone else. No apology. Not even a single 'How you doing, Thandi?' '

'I'm sorry, Thandi. How are you?' Liz asks. Despite appearances, Liz does feel guilty that she's ignored Thandi.

'Fine,' Thandi answers.

'It hasn't been the best time for me,' Liz apologizes.

'You think it's easy for me? You think it's easy for any of us?' Thandi hangs up on Liz.

Liz takes the bus down to the Elsewhere docks. Sure enough, she spots Curtis right away, fishing pole in one hand, cup of coffee in the other. He's wearing a faded red plaid shirt, and his formerly pale skin has a golden hue. His blue hair is almost completely grown out, but his blue eyes remain as vivid as ever. Liz doesn't know if Curtis will remember her. Luckily, he smiles as soon as he sees her.

'Hello, Lizzie,' Curtis says. 'How's the afterlife treating you?' He pours Liz a cup of coffee from a red thermos. He indicates that she should sit next to him on the dock.

'I wanted to ask you a question,' Liz says.

'That sounds serious.' Curtis sits up straighter. 'I shall do my best to answer you, Lizzie.'

'You were honest with me before, back on the boat,' Liz says.

'They say a man should always be as honest as he can.'

Liz lowers her voice. 'I need to make Contact with someone. Can you help me?'

'Are you sure you know what you're doing?'

Liz is prepared for this question and is armed with several appropriate lies. 'I'm not obsessed or anything. I like it here, Curtis. I just have one thing back on Earth that needs taking care of.'

'What is it?' Curtis asks.

'It's something about my death.' Liz hesitates a moment before telling Curtis the whole story of the hit-and-run cabbie.

After she finishes, Curtis is silent for a moment. Then he says, 'I don't know why you thought I would know about this.'

'You seem like a person who knows things,' says Liz. 'Besides, there's no one else I can ask.'

Curtis smiles. 'I have heard that there are two ways to communicate with the living. One, you can try to find a ship back to Earth, although I doubt this would be a very practical solution for you. It takes a long time to get there and, from what I hear, tends to pervert the reverse-aging process. Plus, you don't exactly want to be a ghost, now, do you?'

Liz shakes her head, remembering how she contemplated that very thing on the day she arrived in Elsewhere. 'What's the second way?'

'I have heard of a place, about a mile out to sea and several miles deep. Apparently, this is the deepest place in the ocean. People call it the Well.'

Liz remembers Aldous Ghent mentioning the Well on her first day in Elsewhere. She also remembers him saying that going there was forbidden. 'I think I've heard of it,' she says.

'Supposedly, if you can reach the bottom of this place, a difficult task indeed, you will find a window where you can penetrate to Earth.'

'How is that different from the ODs?' Liz asks.

'The binoculars only go one way. At the Well, they say the living can sense you, see you, hear you.'

'Then I can talk to them?'

'Yes, that's what I've heard,' says Curtis, 'but it will be difficult for them to understand you. Your voice is obscured from being underwater. You need good equipment to make the dive, and even then you should be a good swimmer.'

Liz sips her coffee, contemplating what Curtis has told her. She is a strong swimmer. Last summer she and her mother had even gotten scuba certification together on Cape Cod. Could that have only been a year ago? Liz wonders.

'I'm not sure that I've done the right thing in telling you this information, but you probably would have found out from someone else anyway. I'm afraid I've never been very good at knowing the right thing to do. Or at least knowing it and doing it.'

'Thank you,' Liz says.

'Be careful,' Curtis says. He surprises Liz by hugging her. 'I must ask you, are you sure you should be doing this? Maybe it would be best to leave well enough alone.'

'I have to do this, Curtis. I don't have any choice.'

'Lizzie, my love, there's always a choice.'

Liz doesn't want to argue with Curtis, especially after he's been so nice to her, but she can't help herself. 'I didn't choose to die,' she says, 'so in that instance, there was no choice.'

'No, of course you didn't,' Curtis says. 'I suppose I meant there's always a choice in situations where one has a choice, if that makes any sense.'

'Not really,' Liz says.

'Well, I shall have to work on my philosophy and get back to you, Lizzie. I find there's much time for philosophizing when one fishes for a living.'

Liz nods. As she walks away from the dock, she realizes she forgot to ask Curtis why he had become a fisherman in the first place.

The Big Dive

iz throws herself into preparations for the big dive. Although she hadn't noticed at the time, her daily routine at the Observation Decks had become less and less satisfying: each day blending into the one before it, bleary images that seemed to become blearier and blearier, her eyes strained, her back sore. She now experiences the renewed energy of a person with a *mission*. Liz's walk is faster. Her heart pumps more strongly. Her appetite increases. She rises early and goes to bed late. For the first time since arriving in Elsewhere, Liz feels almost, well, alive.

Curtis had said the Well was "a mile out to sea," but he hadn't specified exactly where. After two days of eavesdropping at the ODs and indirect questioning of Esther, Liz finds out that the Well is thought to be somehow linked to the lighthouses and the ODs and that, to get there, she needs to swim in the path of one of the lighthouses' beams.

To buy the diving equipment, Liz "borrows" another 750 eternims from Betty.

'What do you need them for?' Betty asks.

'Clothes,' Liz lies, although she thinks of her lie as partially true. A wet suit is clothes, right? 'If I'm going to look for an avocation, I'm going to need something to wear.'

'What happened to the last five hundred I gave you?'

'I still have those,' Liz lies again. 'I haven't spent them yet, but I think I'll probably need more. I don't have a single thing except for these pajamas and the T-shirt you got me.'

'Do you want me to come with you?' Betty offers.

'I'd prefer to go on my own,' Liz says.

'I could make you clothes, you know. I *am* a seamstress,' Betty says.

'Mmm, that's a really nice offer, but I think I'd prefer things from the store.'

So Betty relents, although she is fairly certain Liz is lying about what happened to the last five hundred eternims. Betty is doing her best to (1) be patient, and (2) provide Liz a space in which to grieve, and (3) wait for Liz to come to her. This is what it says to do in *How to Talk to Your Recently Deceased Teen*, the book Betty is currently reading. Betty forces a smile. 'I'll drop you off at the East Elsewhere Mall,' she says.

Liz agrees (the dive store is there anyway) but for obvious reasons says she will take the bus back.

The diving tank Liz buys is smaller and lighter than any tank she and her mother ever had on Earth. It's called an Infinity Tank, and the salesman promises Liz that it will never run out of oxygen. As a nod to Betty, Liz also buys one pair of jeans and one long-sleeved T-shirt.

Liz hides the equipment underneath her bed. She feels guilty about lying to Betty but deems the lies necessary evils. She had considered telling Betty about the dive but knew that Betty would only worry. She doesn't need Betty worrying any more than she already does.

It has been a year since Liz's last dive on Earth. She wonders if she will have forgotten all the procedures in the intervening time. She considers making a practice dive, but ultimately decides against it. If she is going to do this, she knows she needs to do it now.

Because going to the Well is forbidden, Liz decides to leave just after sunset. She packs her equipment in a large garbage bag and wears her wet suit under her new jeans and long-sleeved T-shirt.

'Is that what you bought today?' Betty asks.

Liz nods.

'It's nice to see you out of your pajamas.' Betty moves to get a better look at Liz. 'I'm not sure if the fit is right, though.' Betty tries to adjust Liz's T-shirt, but Liz pulls away.

'It's fine!' Liz insists.

'Okay, okay. You'll show me the other things you bought in the morning?'

Liz nods, but looks away.

'Where are you going anyway?' Betty asks.

'That girl Thandi is throwing a party,' Liz lies.

'Well, have a good time!' Betty smiles at Liz. 'What's in the garbage bag, by the way?'

'Just some stuff for the party.' Liz finds telling lies easy now that she's started. The only problem (as many before Liz have discovered) is that she has to keep telling more and more of them.

After Liz has left, Betty decides to go into Liz's room to examine Liz's new clothes. She finds the closet empty, but under the bed she finds a cardboard box with the words INFINITY TANK on it. Remembering Liz's bulky outfit and her big plastic bag, Betty decides to go find her granddaughter. In *How to Talk to Your Recently Deceased Teen*, it also says that you need to know when to *stop* giving your teen space.

Before diving, Liz returns to the OD for a final look at Amadou Bonamy. She wants to see him one last time before turning him in.

From behind her glass box, Esther frowns. 'You haven't been here in a few days. I was hoping you were quit of this place,' she says.

Liz walks past her without answering.

Someone is sitting at Binoculars #15, Liz's usual spot, so she is forced to use #14.

She places a single eternim in the slot and begins to watch Amadou Bonamy. Amadou's cab is vacant, and he's speeding to get somewhere. He parks in front of an elementary school, the same one Liz's brother attends, and runs out of the car. He's walking through the building. He's running through the building. A teacher stands with a small boy wearing glasses at the end of the corridor.

'He threw up in the wastebasket,' the teacher says. 'He didn't want us to call you.'

Amadou gets down on one knee. 'Is it your tummy, my little one?' He speaks with a soft French-Haitian accent.

The boy nods.

'I'll drive you home, *wi bébé*?'

'Don't you have to drive your cab today?' the boy asks.

'*Non, non.* I will make up the fares tomorrow.' Amadou lifts the boy in his arms and winks at the teacher. 'Thank you for calling me.'

The binoculars click closed.

Liz's heart races. She wants to punch someone or break something. Either way, she needs to get out of the Observation Deck immediately.

Outside, the beach is deserted. She takes off her jeans and T-shirt, but she makes no move to get in the water and begin her dive. She just sits, knees to her chest, and thinks about Amadou and his little boy. And the more she thinks about them, the more confused she feels. And the more she thinks about them, the more she wants to stop thinking about them.

Someone calls her name. 'Liz!' It's Betty.

'How did you know I would be here?' Liz asks. She avoids Betty's eyes.

'I didn't. The only place I knew for sure you *wouldn't* be was a party at Thandi's.'

Liz nods.

'That was a joke, by the way.' Betty looks at Liz's wet suit. 'Actually, I found the empty tank box in your room and I thought you might be planning to make Contact.'

'Are you angry?' Liz asks.

'At least I know what you spent the money on,' Betty says.

'That was another joke, by the way. In this book I'm reading, it says that humor is a good way to cope with a difficult situation.'

'What book?' Liz asks.

'It's called *How to Talk to Your Recently Deceased Teen*.'

'Is it helping?'

'Not really.' Betty shakes her head. 'In all seriousness, Liz, I certainly wish you hadn't lied to me, but I'm not angry. I wish you had come to me, but I know it isn't easy for you right now. You probably have your reasons.'

Affected by Betty's words, Liz thinks that Amadou probably had his reasons, too. 'I saw the man who was driving the cab. The cab that hit me, I mean,' Liz says.

'What was he like?'

'He seemed nice.' Liz pauses. 'Did you know I was a hit-and-run?'

'Yes,' Betty replies.

'Why didn't he stop? I mean, if he's a good person. He seems like one.'

'I'm sure he is, Liz. People, you'll find, aren't usually all good or all bad. Sometimes they're a little bit good and a whole lot bad. And sometimes, they're mostly good with a dash of bad. And most of us, well, we fall in the middle somewhere.'

Liz starts to cry, and Betty takes Liz in her arms. All at once, Liz knows she won't tell anyone that Amadou was the driver of the lucky cab—today or any other day. She knows it won't help anything. She suspects that Amadou is a good person. There must have been a good reason he didn't stop. And even if there wasn't, Liz suddenly remembers something else, something that she had not wanted to remember in all this time.

'Betty,' Liz says through tears, 'that day at the mall, I didn't look both ways when I was crossing the street. The traffic light had already turned green, but I didn't see it because I was thinking about something else.'

'What was it?' Betty asks.

'It's so stupid. I was thinking about my watch, how I should have brought it with me to the mall to be repaired. I kept forgetting to do it. I was deciding whether I had enough time to turn around and go back for it, but I couldn't make up my mind, because I didn't know what time it was *because* my watch was broken. It was a big, meaningless circle. Oh Betty, this was my fault. This was all my fault, and now I'm stuck here forever!'

'It only seems like forever,' Betty says gently. 'It's really only fifteen years.'

'It won't make me alive again if he goes to prison,' Liz whispers. 'Nothing can ever do that.'

'So you forgive him?'

'I don't know. I want to, but . . .' Liz's voice trails off. She feels empty. Anger and revenge gave her heft. Without her old friends to prop her up, she's only left with a single question: what now?

'Let's go home,' Betty says. Betty picks up the garbage bag with one hand and brushes the sand off Liz's wet suit with the other.

They take the long way back to the house. The summer air is warm, and Liz's wet suit sticks to her skin.

On one lawn, a boy and a girl run through the sprinklers even though it's after dark.

In a porch swing, a very old man, hunched and shriveled,

holds hands with a beautiful, young redheaded woman. Liz thinks the old man might be the woman's grandfather until she watches the way the pair kisses. *'Te amo,'* the redheaded woman whispers in the old man's ear. She gazes at the old man as if he's the most beautiful person in the world.

On another lawn, two boys of about the same age play catch with a worn-out baseball. 'Should we go in?' the one boy pauses to ask the other.

'No way, Dad,' the other boy answers, 'let's keep playing.'

'Yeah, let's play all night!' the first boy replies.

And so Liz really looks at Betty's street for the first time.

They stop outside Betty's brownstone, which is painted a bold shade of purple. (Strange as it may seem, Liz has never noticed this before.)

The summer air is thick with perfume from Betty's flowers. The scent, Liz thinks, is sweet and melancholy. A bit like dying, a bit like falling in love.

'I'm not going to the ODs anymore, Betty. I'm going to find an avocation, and when I do, I'll pay you back everything, I promise,' Liz says.

Betty looks in Liz's eyes. 'I believe you.' Betty takes Liz's hand in hers. 'And I appreciate that.'

'I'm sorry about the money.' Liz shakes her head. 'All this time, I don't know if you've noticed . . . The thing is, I think I may have been a little *depressed*.'

'I know, doll,' Betty replies, 'I know.'

'Betty,' Liz asks, 'why have you put up with me for so long?'

'At first, for Olivia, I suppose,' Betty answers after a moment's reflection. 'You look so like her.'

'No one wants to be liked for who their mother is, you know,' Liz says.

'I said, at first.'

'So, it wasn't just for Mom's sake, then?'

'Of course not. It was for your own, doll. And mine. Mainly, for mine. I've been lonely for a very long time.'

'Since you came to Elsewhere?'

'Longer than that, I'm afraid.' Betty sighs. 'Did your mother ever tell you why she and I argued?'

'You had an affair,' Liz states, 'and for a long time, Mom wouldn't forgive you.'

'Yes, that's true. I was lonely then, and I've been lonely ever since.'

'Have you considered maybe getting another boyfriend?' Liz asks tactfully.

Betty shakes her head and laughs. 'I'm through with love, at least of the romantic kind. I've lived too long and seen too much.'

'Mom forgave you, you know. I mean, I was named after you, wasn't I?'

'Maybe. I think she just felt sad when I died. And now, I suggest we both go to bed.'

For the first time, Liz sleeps a dreamless sleep. Before, she had always dreamed of Earth.

When she wakes in the morning, Liz calls Aldous Ghent about the position at the Division of Domestic Animals.

Sadie

'Your first real job!' Betty crows. 'How marvelous, doll! Remind me to take your picture when we get there.'

Hearing no response, Betty glances over at Liz in the passenger seat. 'You're certainly quiet this morning,' she says.

'I'm just thinking,' Liz answers. She hopes she won't get fired on her first day.

Aside from the odd babysitting job, Liz never had a 'real job' before. Not that she would have minded having a job. She even offered to get one at the mall when Zooey had, but her parents wouldn't let her. 'School's your job,' her father was fond of saying.

And her mother was in agreement: 'You have your whole life to work.' Liz's mother certainly had been wrong about that one, Liz thinks with a smirk.

What troubles her is this business of speaking Canine. What

if she couldn't pick it up and was fired soon thereafter?

'I remember my first job,' Betty says. 'I was a hatcheck girl at a nightclub in New York City. I was seventeen years old, and I had to lie and say I was eighteen. I made fifty-two dollars a week, which seemed like a great deal of money to me at the time.' Betty smiles at the memory.

As Liz gets out of the car, Betty snaps her picture with an old Polaroid camera. 'Smile, doll!' Betty commands. Liz forces her mouth muscles into a position that she hopes will resemble a smile. 'Have a nice day, Liz! I'll pick you up at five!' Betty waves.

Liz nods tensely. She watches Betty's red car drive away, fighting the urge to run after it. The Division of Domestic Animals is housed in a large A-frame building across the street from the Registry. The building is known as the Barn. Liz knows she has to go inside, but she finds she can't move. She breaks into a sweat, and her stomach feels jittery. Somehow, it reminds her of the first day of school. She takes a deep breath and walks to the entrance. After all, the only way to absolutely ensure things will go badly is to be late.

Liz opens the door. She sees a harried woman with kind green eyes and a mass of frizzy red hair. The woman's denim overalls are covered in a mix of dog hair, cat hair, and what appears to be greenish feathers. She holds out her hand for Liz to shake. 'I'm Josey Wu, the head of the DDA. Are you Aldous's friend Elizabeth?'

'Liz.'

'Hope you don't mind dog hair, Liz.'

'Nah, it's just a little present dogs like to leave behind.'

Josey smiles. 'Well, we've got a lot to do today, Liz, and you can start by changing into these! She tosses Liz a pair of denim overalls.

In the bathroom where Liz changes into the overalls, a medium-sized, rather rangy, blondish dog of indeterminate lineage (in other words, a mutt) is drinking from a toilet.

'Hey, girl,' Liz says to the dog, 'you don't have to drink from there!'

The dog looks up at her. After a moment, the dog cocks her head curiously and speaks. 'Isn't that what it's for?' she asks. 'Why else would they fill a low basin thingy with water? You can even get fresh water by pressing this little handle, right?' The dog demonstrates, flushing the toilet with her left paw.

'No,' says Liz gently, 'it's actually a toilet!'

'Toilet?' the dog asks. 'What's that?'

'Well, it's a place where people go!'

'Go? Go where?'

'Not *where*,' Liz says delicately.

The dog looks at the bowl. 'Good Lord,' she says, 'you mean to say all this time I've been drinking from a place where humans pee and . . . ?' She looks on the verge of throwing up. 'Why didn't anyone ever tell me? I've been drinking from toilets for years. I never knew. They always had the door closed!'

'Here,' says Liz, 'let me get you some fresh water from the sink!' Liz locates a little bowl and fills it with water. 'Here, girl!'

The dog laps up the water excitedly. After she is finished, she licks Liz on the leg. 'Thanks. Now that I'm thinking about it, I think my two-leggers tried to tell me about the whole toilet thing before. My man, Billy he was called, was quite conscientious about shutting the lid! Lick lick lick. 'Had I known, I certainly would have stopped drinking from toilets a long time ago,' she says. 'I'm Sadie, by the way. What are you called?'

'Liz.'

'Nice to meet you, Liz.' Sadie holds out her paw for Liz to shake. 'I just died last week. It's weird here.'

'How did you die?' Liz asks.

'I was chasing a ball and I got hit by a car,' Sadie says.

'I was hit by a car, too,' says Liz, 'only I was on a bike.'

'Did you have a dog?' Sadie wants to know.

'Oh yes, Lucy was my best friend in the whole world.'

'You want a new dog?' Sadie cocks her head.

'You mean you, don't you, girl?' Liz asks.

Sadie lowers her head shyly.

'I don't know if my grandmother will let me, but I'll ask tonight, all right?'

Josey enters the bathroom. 'Great, Liz, I'm glad to see you met Sadie,' Josey says as she scratches the dog between the ears. 'Sadie is your first advisee.'

Sadie nods her soft yellow head.

'Aldous didn't mention you speak Canine, by the way,' Josey says.

'About that,' Liz stammers, 'I don't.'

'What do you mean?' asks Josey. 'I just heard you have a whole conversation with Sadie.'

And then it dawns on Liz. She was *speaking* to Sadie.

Liz grins. 'I've never spoken it before. Or at least, I never knew I was.'

'Well, looks like you're a natural. Remarkable! I've only met a handful of natural Canine speakers in my whole life. You're sure you weren't taught somewhere?'

Liz shakes her head. 'I just always seemed to understand dogs, and they always seemed to understand me.' She thinks of Lucy. She thinks of that dog in the park. 'I never knew it was a language, though. I never knew it was a skill.'

'Well, looks like you were destined to work here, Liz,' Josey says, patting Liz on the back. 'Come on, let's step into my office. If you'll excuse us, Sadie.'

Sadie looks at Liz. 'You'll remember to ask your grandmother, right?'

'I promise.' Liz scratches Sadie between the ears and leaves the bathroom.

'So, as a counselor for the Division of Domestic Animals, your job basically entails explaining to the new dog arrivals everything about life on Elsewhere and then placing them in new homes. For some of the dogs, speaking to you will be the first conversation they've ever had with a human. It can get rather hairy, in both senses of the word.' This is obviously not the first time Josey has made this joke.

'Is it very difficult?' Liz asks.

'Not really. Dogs are a lot more flexible than humans, and even though we don't always understand dogs, dogs understand us pretty well,' Josey replies. 'Since you already speak Canine, you're halfway there, Liz. Everything else you can learn as you go along.'

'What about other animals?' Liz asks.

'As a DDA counselor, you'll mainly deal in dogs, of course, but within our division, we also deal with all household pets:

cats, some pigs, the occasional snake, guinea pigs, and so on. The fish are the worst; they die so quickly, they spend most of their time just swimming back and forth.'

At that moment Sadie pokes her head into Josey's office. 'You haven't forgotten, right?'

'No, but I'm sort of busy right now, Sadie,' Liz answers. Sadie lowers her head and slinks out the door.

Josey laughs, then whispers, 'You know, you can't take all the dogs home with you.'

'I heard that!' Sadie calls out from the other room.

'And you'll find they all have excellent hearing,' Josey says. 'Let's find you an office, Liz.'

After Sadie, Liz's next advisee is an insecure little Chihuahua named Paco.

'But where's Pete?' Paco asks, his intense little eyes darting around Liz's new windowless office.

'I'm sorry, but you probably won't see Pete anytime soon. He's still on Earth,' Liz says to Paco.

'Do you think Pete's mad at me?' Paco asks. 'I sometimes pee in his shoes when he leaves me home alone too long, but I don't think he notices. Maybe he notices? Do you think he notices? I'm a bad, bad, bad dog.'

'I'm sure Pete isn't mad at you. You can't see him because you died.'

'Oh,' says Paco softly.

Finally, Liz thinks to herself. 'Do you understand now?' Liz asks.

'I think so,' says Paco, 'but where's Pete?'

Liz sighs. After a moment, she begins her explanation one more time. 'You know, Paco, for the longest time, I wasn't sure where I was either . . .'

When Liz leaves work that night, Sadie follows her to Betty's car.

'Who's this?' Betty asks.

'This is Sadie,' Liz says. And then she lowers her voice. 'Is it all right?'

Sadie looks expectantly at Betty.

Betty smiles. 'Seems like Sadie's already made up her mind.' Sadie licks Betty's face. 'Oy! Welcome to the family, Sadie. I'm Betty.'

'Hi, Betty!' Sadie hops into the backseat. 'Did I tell you that I was named for a Beatles song? My full name's Sexy Sadie, actually, but you don't have to call me Sexy unless you want to. I mean, it's a little presumptuous, don't you think?'

'What's she saying?' Betty asks Liz.

'Sadie says she's named after some Beatles song,' Liz translates.

'Oh sure, I know that song.' Betty sings, '*Sexy Sadie, what have you done*? Or something like that, right?'

'That's the song!' Sadie says. 'That's exactly it!' She places a paw on Betty's shoulder. 'Betty, you're a genius!' Sadie barks a few bars of the song.

Liz laughs again, a pretty, twinkly laugh.

'What a lovely laugh you have, Liz,' Betty says. 'I'm not sure I've ever heard it before.'

The Well

Despite her modest salary at the DDA, Liz quickly pays back all of Betty's eternims. She soon finds she has a great deal of spare ones and nothing really to spend them on. She lives with Betty and pays a small amount for her room and board; she doesn't need health insurance or car insurance (unfortunately) or renter's insurance or any other sort of insurance; she doesn't have to save for a down payment on a house or retirement or college or her children's college or a lavish wedding or a rainy day or anything else. She doesn't go to the OD anymore. She would buy a car, but what would be the point when she can't drive anyway? When you aren't preparing for old age, senility, sickness, death, or children, there is relatively little to spend on, Liz thinks with a sigh.

'Aldous,' Liz asks during her monthly progress meeting, 'what am I supposed to do with all these eternims?'

'Buy something nice,' Aldous suggests.

'Like what?'

Aldous shrugs. 'A house?'

'I don't need a house. I live with Betty,' Liz answers. 'What is the point of going to work if I don't really need the eternims anyway?'

'You go to work,' Aldous pauses, 'because you like it. That's why we call it an avocation.'

'Oh, I see.'

'You do like your work, don't you, Elizabeth?'

'No,' Liz answers after a moment's reflection, 'I love it.'

It had been just over a month since Liz began her avocation. In that time, she had become known as one of the best counselors at the Division of Domestic Animals. She was in that rare and enviable situation: she excelled at her work, and she loved doing it. Work helped the rest of her first summer in Elsewhere pass quickly. Work took her mind off the fact that she was dead.

She worked long hours, and what little time was left, she spent with Betty, Sadie, or Thandi. (Liz apologized to Thandi not long after she started at the DDA, and was quickly forgiven.) Liz tried not to think about her mother or her father or her old life on Earth. For the most part, she was successful.

Liz even convinced Thandi to adopt the confused Chihuahua Paco. Initially, Thandi was skeptical. 'You sure it's a dog? Looks more like a little rat to me.'

Paco was skeptical, too. 'I don't mean to be rude,' he said, 'but why aren't you Pete?'

'I'm Thandi. You can think of me as New Pete.'

'Oh,' said Paco thoughtfully, 'I think I finally understand. You're saying *Pete* died. Is that it?' Paco had drowned in a kiddie pool, which he had apparently forgotten again.

'Sure, you can think of it that way if it suits you.' Thandi patted Paco gingerly on the head.

Many nights after work, the two girls walk Paco and Sadie in the park near Liz's house. On one of those evenings, Liz asks Thandi, 'Are you happy?'

'No point in being sad, Liz.' Thandi shrugs. 'The weather's nice here, and I like being on TV.'

'Do you remember when I thought everything was a dream?' Liz asks. 'I can't believe I ever thought that, because now it seems like everything on Earth, everything that came before . . . It sometimes seems like that was the dream.'

Thandi nods.

'Sometimes,' Liz says, 'I wonder if this is all there is. Just our jobs, walking the dogs, and that's it.'

'What's wrong with this?' Thandi asks.

'It's just, don't you ever long for a bit of adventure, Thandi? A bit of romance?'

'Wasn't dying enough of an adventure for you, Liz?' Thandi shakes her head. 'Personally, I've had just about all the adventure I can take.'

'Yes,' Liz answers finally, 'I suppose you're right.'

'I think you're already on an adventure, and you don't even know it,' Thandi says.

And yet one thing tugs at Liz's mind. Liz's father's forty-fifth birthday is the week after next. Several months before his birthday, Liz had been in the Lord & Taylor's Men's Department with

Zooey. While Zooey had been comparing silk boxer shorts to buy for her boyfriend John on Valentine's Day (tiny glow-in-the dark cupids? Pairs of polar bears locked in perpetual kisses?), Liz had spotted a sea green cashmere sweater that was the exact color of her father's eyes. The sweater cost $150, but it was absolutely perfect. Liz had the money saved from several months of babysitting. The logic part of her brain had begun to protest. It's nowhere near your father's birthday, it said. It's a bit extravagant, it insisted. Maybe you could get Mom to pay for it, it taunted. Liz had ignored the voice. She knew if she didn't buy the sweater right then, it probably wouldn't be there when she went back for it. (It had never occurred to Liz that *she* might not be there.) Besides, she hadn't wanted her mother to buy it; she had wanted to buy it herself. There was something more honest about it that way. She had taken a deep breath, plunked the money on the counter, and bought the sweater. As soon as she got home from the mall, she had wrapped the sweater and written out a card. She had hidden the package in the narrow space underneath a loose floorboard in her closet, where she was quite confident no one would ever find it.

Of all the things that could be bothering Liz, the thought that her father might never receive the sweater irrationally torments her. Her father would never know that she would spend $150 of her *own money* on him. Her father might move from their house never finding her gift, never knowing that Liz had loved him enough to buy him the perfect sea green sweater. It would remain hidden, eventually attracting moths and deteriorating into unidentifiable shreds of perfect sea green cashmere. A sweater that beautiful, Liz thinks, is not meant for such a tragic end.

She knows that Contact is illegal, yet she refuses to believe that getting one insignificant sweater to her father could really cause that much trouble. If anything, she is sure it will facilitate her father in the grieving process.

And so for the second time, Liz decides to dive to the Well. She already has the equipment, and this time she actually has a good reason. Besides, life is better with a little adventure.

Liz arrives at the beach at sunset. The dive to the Well is the most ambitious one Liz has ever attempted. She doesn't know exactly how deep it will be or what she'll find when she gets to the lowest point. Liz pushes those concerns to the back of her mind. She checks the gauge on her Infinity Tank one last time and begins to swim.

The deeper Liz dives, the darker the water becomes. All around her, she senses the presence of other people. Presumably, they are also going to the Well. Occasionally, she discerns indistinct shapes or odd rustlings, lending her descent an eerie, almost haunted feeling.

Finally, Liz reaches the Well. It is the saddest, quietest place she has ever been. It looks like an open drain at the bottom of a sink. Intense light pours out of the opening. Liz peers over the edge, into the light. She can see her house on Carroll Drive. The house appears faded, like a watercolor painting left in the sun. In the kitchen, Liz's family is just sitting down to dinner.

Liz speaks into the Well. Her voice sounds garbled from

being underwater. She knows she has to choose her words carefully, if she is to be understood. 'THIS IS LIZ. LOOK UNDER THE CLOSET FLOORBOARDS. THIS IS LIZ. LOOK UNDER THE CLOSET FLOORBOARDS.'

At Liz's old house, all the faucets simultaneously turn on: every shower and every sink, the dishwasher, even the toilet gurgles. Liz's family looks at one another, perplexed. Lucy barks insistently. 'That's odd,' Liz's mother says, getting up to turn off the kitchen sink.

'Must be something wrong with the plumbing,' Liz's father adds before going to turn off the shower and the bathroom sink.

Only Alvy remains at the table. He hears the faintest high-pitched something coming from the faucets, though he isn't able to identify what it is. From the Well, Liz watches him push his hair back behind his ears. His hair is so long, Liz thinks. Why hasn't anyone cut his hair?

Having turned off all the faucets, Liz's mother and father return to the table. About five seconds later, the water starts up all over again.

'Well, I'll be damned,' Liz's father says, standing to turn off the water for the second time.

Liz's mother is about to stand when suddenly Alvy pushes his chair away from the table. 'STOP!' he yells.

'What is it?' Liz's mother asks.

'Be quiet,' Alvy says with remarkable authority for a person of eight, 'and please don't touch the sink.'

'Why?' Liz's parents ask the question in unison.

'It's Lizzie,' Alvy says quietly. 'I think I can hear Lizzie.'

At this point, Liz's mother begins to sob. Liz's father looks at Alvy. 'Is this some kind of a joke?' he asks.

Alvy puts his ear up to the spigot. He can just make out Liz's voice.

'ALVY, IT'S LIZ. THERE'S SOMETHING FOR DAD UNDER THE FLOORBOARDS IN MY CLOSET.'

Alvy nods. 'I'll tell him, Lizzie. Are you okay?'

Liz doesn't get a chance to answer. At that moment, a net falls over her, and she is pulled back toward the surface.

Thrashing her arms and legs, Liz attempts to free herself. Her efforts are for naught. The more she struggles, the tighter the net seems to become. Liz quickly realizes the futility of trying to escape. She sighs, accepting her momentary defeat gracefully. At least the ascent to shore will be quicker than if she had to swim it herself.

The net propels Liz upward with astonishing speed, almost like a waterslide in reverse. At first, Liz is concerned that she might get the bends. She soon realizes that the net seems to be providing its own pressurization system. How odd, thinks Liz, that Elsewhere has advanced netting technology. What makes a civilization develop sophisticated nets? she wonders. Maybe it's the– Liz forces all thoughts of nets from her mind and tries to focus on the situation at hand.

Despite being captured, Liz is in high spirits. She is reasonably sure that her mission has been a success. Of course, no one had prepared her for the odd way one communicated from the Well: all the loud faucets, Liz's disembodied voice like an irate teapot. Is this what it means to be a ghost?

Liz latches her fingers into the netting. She wonders where

she is being taken. Clearly, her little trip has gotten her into some sort of trouble. But all things considered, she is glad she went.

As she reaches the surface, Liz braces herself for the cool night air. Even in her expensive wet suit, she begins to shiver. Liz pulls off her diving mask and sees a white tugboat in the middle of the water. She can barely make out a dark-haired man standing on the deck. As she is drawn closer, Liz can see that he is wearing sunglasses even though it is night. She determines that he is probably older than her, but younger than Curtis Jest. (Of course, determining actual ages is a particularly tricky business in Elsewhere.) The man seems familiar, but Liz can't quite place him.

The net opens, and Liz is unceremoniously dumped onto the boat. As soon as she hits the deck, the man begins to speak to her in a stern voice: 'Elizabeth Marie Hall, I am Detective Owen Welles of the Elsewhere Bureau of Supernatural Crime and Contact. Are you aware that by attempting to Contact the living, you are in violation of Elsewhere law?'

'Yes,' Liz says in a strong voice.

Owen Welles appears to be taken aback by Liz's response. This woman, girl really, freely admits that she has broken the law. Most people at least try to dissemble.

'Would you mind taking off those sunglasses?' Liz asks.

'Why?'

'I want to see your eyes. I want to know how much trouble I'm in.' Liz smiles.

Detective Owen Welles is somewhat defensive about his sunglasses. He never goes anywhere without them, because he believes they make him look more authoritative. And why is she smiling?

'You can't actually need sunglasses right now,' Liz says. 'It is night, after all.'

Liz is starting to annoy Owen. He hates when people mention that he wears his sunglasses at night. Now, he definitely won't take them off.

'Owen Welles,' Liz repeats the name aloud. 'O. Welles, like "Oh well"!' Liz begins to laugh, even though she knows her joke isn't a particularly good one.

'Right, I've never heard that before.' Owen does not laugh.

'Oh well,' Liz says, and then she laughs again. 'Isn't it odd that your last name should be Welles, and you happen to work at the Well?'

'What's odd about that?' Owen demands.

'Not so much odd as coincidental, I suppose,' Liz says. 'Um, can I just get my punishment or my ticket or whatever, and get out of here?'

'I have to show you something first. Follow me,' he says.

Owen leads Liz across the main deck to a telescope that is mounted at the stern. 'Look,' he orders Liz.

Liz obeys. The telescope works much like the binoculars on the Observation Decks. Through the eyepiece, Liz sees inside her house again. Her brother is kneeling in her parents' closet, his hands feeling frantically for loose floorboards. Alvy keeps mumbling to himself, 'She said it was in your closet.'

'Oh no!' Liz exclaims. 'He's in the wrong closet. Alvy, it's in *my* closet!'

'He can't hear you,' Owen says.

Through the telescope Liz can see her father yelling at poor Alvy. 'Get out of there!' her father screams, pulling Alvy by his shirt collar so hard that it rips. 'Why are you making up stories about Lizzie? She's dead, and I won't have you making up stories!'

Alvy starts to cry.

'He's not making it up! He just misunderstood.' Liz feels her heart racing.

'I'm not making it up,' Alvy protests. 'Liz told me to. She told me to—' Alvy stops speaking as Liz's father raises his hand to slap Alvy across the face.

'NO!' Liz yells.

'They can't hear you, Miss Hall,' Owen says.

At the last moment, Liz's father stops himself. He takes a deep breath and slowly lowers his hand. Liz watches as her father slumps to the floor and begins to sob. 'Oh, Lizzie,' he sobs, 'Lizzie! My poor Lizzie! Lizzie!'

The telescope image blurs and then turns black. Liz takes a step back.

'My father doesn't believe in hitting,' she says, her voice barely above a whisper, 'and he almost hit Alvy.'

'Now do you see?' asks Owen gently.

'Now do I see what?'

'It isn't any good to talk to the living, Liz. You think you're helping, but you only make matters worse.'

Suddenly, Liz turns on Owen. 'This is all your fault!' she says.

'My fault?'

'I might have made Alvy understand if you hadn't pulled me

140

away before I was finished explaining!' Liz takes a step closer to Owen. 'In fact, I want you to take me back now!'

'As if I'm really going to do that. Honestly. What nerve.'

'If you won't help me, I'll do it myself!' Liz runs to the side of the tugboat. Owen chases after her, restraining her from diving overboard.

'LET ME GO!' she says. But Owen is stronger than Liz, and she has already had a long day. All at once, Liz feels very tired.

'I'm sorry,' says Owen. 'I'm really sorry, but this is the way it has to be.'

'Why?' asks Liz. 'Why does it have to be this way?'

'Because the living have to get on with their lives, and the dead have to get on with their lives, too.'

Liz shakes her head.

Owen removes his sunglasses, revealing sympathetic dark eyes framed in long dark lashes. 'If it matters,' says Owen, 'I know how you feel. I died young, too.'

Liz looks at Owen's face. Without his sunglasses, she determines he is only a little older than her, probably around seventeen or eighteen. 'How old were you when you got here?'

Owen pauses. 'Twenty-six.'

Twenty-six, Liz thinks bitterly. There is a world of difference between twenty-six and fifteen. Twenty-six does things that fifteen only dreams of. When Liz finally speaks, it is in the melancholy voice of a person much older than her years. 'I'm fifteen years old, Mr. Welles. I will never turn sixteen, and before long, I'll be fourteen again. I won't go to the prom, or college, or Europe, or anywhere else. I won't ever get a Massachussetts driver's license or a high school diploma. I won't ever live with anyone who's not my grandmother. I don't think you know how I feel.'

'You're right,' Owen says softly. 'I only meant it's difficult for all of us to get on with our lives.'

'I am getting on with my life,' Liz says. 'I just had this one thing I needed to do. I doubt it would have made any difference to anyone except me, but I needed to do it.'

'What was it?' Owen asks.

'Why should I tell you?'

'It's for the report I have to file,' Owen says. Of course, this is only partially true.

Liz sighs. 'If you must know, there was this sweater, a sea green cashmere one, hidden beneath the floorboards of my closet. It was a birthday present for my dad. The color, it matched his eyes.'

'A sweater?' Owen is incredulous.

'What's wrong with a sweater?' Liz demands.

'No offense, but most people who bother to make the trip to the Well have more important things to do.' Owen shakes his head.

'It was important to me,' Liz insists.

'I mean, like life-or-death sorts of things. The location of buried bodies, the name of a murderer, wills, money. You get my drift.'

'Sorry, but nothing of much importance ever happened to me,' Liz says. 'I'm just a girl who forgot to look both ways before she crossed the street.'

A foghorn sounds, indicating that the tugboat has reached the marina.

'So, am I in trouble?' Liz tries to keep her voice light.

'As it was only your first offense, mainly all you get is a warning. It goes without saying that I have to tell your acclimation counselor. Yours is Aldous Ghent, correct?'

Liz nods.

'Good man, Ghent is. For the next six weeks, you're banned from any Observation Decks, and I have to confiscate your diving gear during that time.'

'Fine,' Liz says haughtily. 'I can go, then?'

'If you go down to the Well again, there will be serious consequences. I wouldn't want to see you get into any trouble, Miss Hall.'

Liz nods.

As she is walking to the bus stop, she thinks about Alvy and her father and all the trouble she caused for her family. Heartsick and slightly damp, she realizes that Owen Welles was probably right. He must think I'm so stupid, Liz says to herself.

Of course, Owen Welles thinks nothing of the kind.

The people who worked for the bureau were, more often than not, those who had the most trouble accepting their own deaths. Although these individuals had great empathy for the lawbreakers, they understood all too well the need to be firm with the first-time Contacter. It was a dangerous thing to slip into casual Contact with the living.

So it is somewhat unusual that Owen Welles finds himself wondering about that sea green cashmere sweater. He isn't sure why. He supposes it is because Liz's request was so specific. Most people who visited the Well needed to be stopped for their own good, or they would become obsessed with people on Earth. Somehow, this didn't seem to be the case with Liz.

What would it have hurt, really, for her father to get that sweater? Owen asks himself. It might have made things a little easier for parents who had outlived their child and a lovely girl who had died too young.

A Piece of String

In times of stress Liz would instinctively stroke the stitches over her ear, and the evening's journey to the Well had certainly ended up being stressful. That night in bed, Liz discovers that her stitches are gone. For the first time in months, Liz sobs and sobs.

She supposes they must have fallen out during the dive—probably some combination of the intense pressure and all the water. Liz feels desperate that her last piece of Earth is gone forever. She even considers taking another dive to search for the string. She quickly dismisses the idea. First, she is forbidden from diving, and second, even if she weren't forbidden from diving, the string (actually a polyester thread) is less than three inches long and one-sixteenth of an inch thick. It would be insanity to try to find it.

Liz runs her pinky across the scar where the string used to

be. She can barely feel it. She knows the scar will soon be gone, too. And when that happens, it will be like she was never on Earth at all.

Liz laughs. All these tears over a piece of string, and all this drama over a sweater. Her life came down to a spool of thread. Now that she thinks about it, she isn't completely sure *when* she lost the stitches. Since starting her avocation, she hadn't needed to touch them so much. Actually, she can't even remember the last time she touched them before tonight. They might have been gone for a while (what if they had been the dissolving kind?), and maybe she hadn't even noticed? Liz laughs again.

At the sound of Liz's laughter, Betty pokes her head into Liz's room. 'Is something funny? I could use a good joke.'

'I was arrested,' Liz says with a laugh.

Betty starts to laugh and then stops. She turns on Liz's bedroom light. 'You're not serious.'

'I am. Illegal dive to the Well. I was trying to Contact Dad.' Liz shrugs.

'Liz!'

'Don't worry, Betty, I learned my lesson. It totally wasn't worth the trip,' Liz says. 'I'll tell you the whole story.'

Betty sits on Liz's bed. After Liz is finished, Betty says, 'People drown out there, you know. No one ever finds them. They just lie on the bottom of the ocean, half dead.'

'You don't have to worry about me drowning, because I'm never going back,' Liz says firmly. 'The worst part of it is that Alvy's final memory will be me lying to him and getting him in trouble. If he wasn't going to find the sweater anyway, I just wish I'd said, 'Hey, Alvy, you're a great brother, and I love you.' '

'He knows that, Liz,' Betty replies.

Liz reaches for her stitches, but of course they aren't there. 'Betty,' Liz asks, 'how do you stop missing Earth?'

'You don't,' Betty replies.

'So it's hopeless?' Liz sighs.

'Now I didn't say that, did I?' Betty admonishes Liz. 'Here's what you do. Make a list of all the things you really miss about Earth. Think really hard. It can't just be a bunch of names, either. Because those are people you miss, and we have plenty of people here, too.'

'Yes, so I make a list. Then what?'

'Then either you throw the list away and accept that you're never going to have those things again, or you go about getting everything back.'

'How do I get anything back?' Liz asks.

'I wish I knew,' Betty says.

'Well, how long should the list be?'

'Oh, I'd limit yourself to three or four things. Five tops.'

'You're just making this up as you go along, aren't you?'

'You asked my advice, remember!' Betty says. 'And now we both ought to go to sleep.'

Betty walks to the door, stopping to turn off Liz's bedroom light.

'Hey, Betty?' Liz calls out. 'Thank you.'

'For what, doll?'

'For . . .' Liz's voice trails off. 'You're really not bad at this whole grandmother thing, after all,' Liz whispers.

The next day at work, Liz makes her list.

The Things I Miss Most from Earth
by Elizabeth M. Hall
1)   Bagels & lox with Mom, Dad, & Alvy on Sunday
     morning
2)   The Feeling that Something Good Might Be Right
     around the Corner
3)   Various smells: the sweet cookie smell of Mom, the
     acrid, stingy, soapy smell of Dad, the yeasty breadlike
     smell of Alvy
4)   My pocket watch

Liz reads over her list. Seeing it all written down, she isn't sure what to make of it. Do I throw it out, or do I try to get everything back? Can you possibly do a combination of both?

Or, Liz thinks, was Betty just playing with her?

Liz has her answer. She laughs and throws the list away.

For a moment, Liz considers her pocket watch. It was strange that she had barely thought of her watch since coming to Elsewhere. The watch had been her father's before it was hers, and for years she had coveted it. Two lovers in a gondola were etched on the front, and her father's initials, A.S.H., were engraved on the inside. The watch made a peculiarly pleasing ticking sound, almost like a very low bell, and the silver was so frequently polished it was the color of the moon. On her thirteenth birthday, her dad had said she was old enough to have the watch and he had given it to her. He made her promise to always clean and maintain it. About a month before she died, the watch had stopped, and she still feels guilty about not getting it repaired. She hates to imagine her father finding it broken and thinking that Liz hadn't cared about it at all.

Owen Welles Takes a Dive

Owen Welles was born to a college professor mother and a painter father in New York City. His parents were consistently delighted by their only child, a smiling, verbal, good-looking boy. Owen's childhood passed easily and without trauma. When he was thirteen, he met the red-haired Emily Reilly, also thirteen. Emily was quite literally the girl next door. Owen lived in Apartment 7C, Emily in 7D. Owen and Emily shared a bedroom wall, and they would tap Morse code to each other late at night when they were both supposed to be asleep. It wasn't long before Owen went the way of many a boy next door: he fell in love with Emily. A series of proms and other photo opportunities followed, leading right up to high school graduation.

Following graduation, Emily went to college in Massachusetts, while Owen stayed for college in New York City. After four years of exorbitant long-distance bills, they were married at twenty-two. In a bout of traditionalism that surprised everyone concerned, Emily even took Owen's last name. Emily Reilly became Emily Welles.

To save money, Owen and Emily moved to Brooklyn. Emily went to medical school, and Owen became a firefighter. He wasn't sure if he wanted to be a firefighter forever, but he liked his work and was good at it.

In the year Owen turned twenty-six, he was killed fighting the most routine fire in the world. An eighty-one-year-old woman left a burner on; her four cats were trapped in the apartment. Owen located the first three cats easily, but the fourth, a young white tom called Koshka, eluded him. Unaware of the fire, the cat had fallen asleep in a closet. Owen didn't find Koshka until the next morning. The cat was happily licking his paws at the foot of Owen's bunk on the *Nile*. Both he and Koshka had been asphyxiated. 'I'm thirsty', the cat meowed. Unfortunately, Owen did not speak Catus.

Owen did not take his death well. It is much harder to die when one is in love.

Because of Emily, he did everything he could to get back to Earth. He tried to take the boat back, but he was discovered before it left the seaport.

He wasn't the first person to become addicted to the binoculars at the Observation Deck. Exhausting an enormous supply of borrowed coins, Owen would watch Emily until his eyes glazed over.

He attempted the illegal deep-sea dive to the Well a record 117 times. He sometimes managed to communicate with Emily, but mainly he drove her insane. She missed Owen intensely, and his semiregular visits only made things worse. Emily dropped out of medical school. She just stayed at home, waiting for Owen to come back. Eventually, Owen realized what he was doing to her, and he knew he had to stop. He didn't want to be responsible for ruining her life. Because of Owen's experience with illegal Contact, he seemed a natural to work for the Bureau.

Now seventeen years old, Owen had worked at the bureau for nine years. Owen didn't have many friends and had only a few relatives he rarely saw. Once a week (never more, never less), he allowed himself to watch Emily from the binoculars. Every Thursday night he saw Emily grow older as he grew younger. At thirty-five years old, Emily was now a burn specialist. (She went back to medical school the fall after Owen's death.) She never remarried and still wore her wedding band. Owen wore a wedding band, too. He had bought a new one on Elsewhere to replace the one he had left behind on Earth.

At a certain point Owen realized that he would probably never see Emily again. He had done the math. In all probability, by the time Emily reached Elsewhere, Owen would be back on Earth. He had learned to live with this fact, but even ten years down the road, the only person for him was Emily Reilly.

When people asked him if he was married, Owen told them he was. This statement seemed like a lie and the truth at the same time. Not surprisingly, Owen often felt like a fraud. How could he advise other people to do what he had never been able to do himself? When he met a person like Liz, he was particularly ashamed. In his opinion, she legitimately wanted to move on and he had hindered her in that process. Owen felt the need to make amends.

And so, Owen takes a dive into the Well, his first dive for a personal reason in many years.

He peers over the Well's edge and quickly locates Liz's house in Medford, Massachusetts. Owen finds Alvy, sitting at the kitchen table, drinking a glass of apple juice.

Because Owen has made so many dives before, he is quite sophisticated at making Contact. Consequently, when Owen speaks through the Well, only one faucet comes on at Liz's old house.

'Hello,' says Owen.

Alvy sighs. 'You've got the wrong house. The only dead person I know is my sister, Lizzie.'

'I know Liz, too.'

'Yeah,' says Alvy, 'if you see her, tell her I'm mad. I didn't find anything in the closet, and I got in big trouble.'

'You were in the wrong closet,' says Owen. 'It's under the floorboards in *Liz's* closet.'

Alvy sets down his glass. 'Say, who are you anyway?'

'I guess you could say I'm a friend of Liz's. She's sorry she got you in trouble, by the way.'

'Well, tell her I miss her,' Alvy says. 'She was a pretty good sister, most of the time. Oh, and tell her Happy Thanksgiving, too.'

Liz's father enters the kitchen. He turns off the faucet. 'Why did you leave this running again?' Liz's father asks Alvy.

'It just came on by itself,' Alvy replies. 'And Dad? Please don't get mad, but I have to show you something in Liz's closet.'

Owen stays to watch Alvy lead Liz's father up the stairs. He watches as Alvy opens a loose floorboard on the left side. He watches Alvy pull out a foil-wrapped box with a card on the front that reads, TO DAD.

When Owen surfaces an hour later, his colleagues from the bureau are waiting for him.

'I just thought you'd like to know he got the sweater.' Owen stands awkwardly in front of Liz's desk at work the night before Thanksgiving. Although Thanksgiving isn't an official holiday in Elsewhere, many Americans still celebrate it anyway.

'You went to the Well for me?'

'Your brother . . . Alvy, is it?'

Liz nods.

'Alvy says "Happy Thanksgiving." ' Owen turns to leave.

'Wait!' Liz grabs Owen's arm. 'Wait a minute, you can't just go!' Liz pulls Owen into a hug. 'Thank you.'

'You're welcome,' Owen says gruffly.

'Did he like the sweater?' Liz asks.

'He loved it. It matched his eyes just like you said it would.' As Owen says this, he realizes the sweater matched Liz's eyes also.

Liz sits down in her desk chair. 'I really don't know how to thank you.'

'It's just part of my job.'

'It's part of your job to give my dad a sweater?'

'Well, not technically,' Owen admits.

'What else did Alvy say?'

'He said you were a good sister. Actually, he said you were a good sister most of the time.'

Liz laughs and grabs Owen by the hand. 'Come to Thanksgiving dinner at my house. Well, it's Betty's house and my house. Betty's my grandmother.'

'I . . .' Owen looks away.

'Of course,' Liz says, 'this late, you probably have other plans.'

Owen thinks a moment. He never has other plans. He typically eschews holidays like Thanksgiving, holidays spent among other people's loved ones. Even after ten years, making other plans somehow feels like betraying Emily. Normally, Owen eats alone at a diner with a holiday special. 'It's a strange thing about Thanksgiving,' Owen says finally. 'I mean, why do so many of us still celebrate it over here anyway? Is it just habit? Are we just doing it because we always have?'

'Listen, you don't have to come if—'

Owen interrupts her. 'And people barely think about the whole Pilgrims-and-Indians thing over there, and it really has absolutely nothing to do with anything over here. And yet right around Thanksgiving, despite myself, I always get that Thanksgiving feeling and want to make amends and eat pie. It's conditioned in me. Why is that?'

'I know what you mean. This last September, I still wanted to buy school supplies even though I don't go to school anymore,' Liz says. 'Although, it's a little different with Thanksgiving. I think it's just something you can do to be like the people back home. Or to be close to the people back home. You eat pie because you know they're eating pie.'

Owen nods. All this talk of pie has suddenly put Owen in the mood for just that. 'So,' he says casually, 'what time should I get there?'

Thanksgiving

I hope you don't mind, but I've invited another person,' Liz announces to Betty that night. Liz has already invited Aldous Ghent and his wife, Rowena; Thandi, her cousin Shelly, and Paco the Chihuahua; and several of her advisees at the DDA. She had also invited Curtis Jest, but he declined on the grounds that he was an Englishman and found the holiday "rather maudlin" anyway.

'The more the merrier,' says Betty. On Earth, Betty had been fond of holidays, and her fondness only intensified in the after-life. 'Who is it?' Betty asks.

'Owen Welles.'

'You don't mean that awful boy who gave you all the trouble at the Well?' Betty asks. Liz's "episode with the law" (as Betty calls it) is a continuing sore spot for Betty.

'That's the one,' Liz replies.

'I thought you didn't like him,' Betty says, raising her left eyebrow.

'I don't, not really. But he did me a favor, and I got caught up in the moment.' Liz sighs. 'The truth is, Betty, I didn't imagine that he'd say yes. And then I was stuck, because I couldn't exactly un-invite him, now could I?'

'No,' Betty agrees and laughs. 'So, who's next, Liz? Maybe you'd like to invite a retired axe murderer?'

'I'll see if I can find one.' Liz laughs, too. 'Say, do we even have those here?'

As on Earth, or at least in the United States, Thanksgiving falls on a Thursday.

Aldous and Rowena Ghent arrive first, followed by Thandi and Shelly, who bring pies, and Paco in a turkey suit to commemorate the occasion.

The last to arrive is Owen Welles. He spent the morning inventing good reasons to cancel (septic-tank explosion? emergency at work?). At the last possible moment, he decides to go anyway. These days, he has a bit of free time on his hands, having been suspended for a month on account of the sweater dive. He brings a potted plant for Liz's grandmother.

Aside from the presence of dead people, Thanksgiving on Elsewhere is like Thanksgiving pretty much anywhere else they celebrate it. While she loves holidays, Betty doesn't love cooking. She has the meal catered, coincidentally from the same diner Owen usually went to for the special. Betty serves cranberry sauce (canned and homemade), potatoes (mashed and sweet), cornbread stuffing, gravy, small yeasty rolls, green bean casserole, stuffed mushrooms, Thandi and Shelly's four pies (apple, pecan, pumpkin, and sweet potato), and tofurkey (which is a vegetarian turkey substitute and definitely an acquired taste).

Betty pours large tumblers of white wine for everyone. Although Liz has had wine before, it is the first time she has ever been served wine by Betty and it makes her feel grown-up somehow.

After the wine is poured, Betty says, 'I'd like to make a short toast.' She clears her throat, 'Well, we've all had to travel a long way to get here.' She pauses.

'Hear! Hear!' Aldous says.

'I'm not finished yet,' Betty says.

'Oh, excuse me,' Aldous apologizes. 'I thought you said a short toast.'

'Not *that* short,' Betty protests.

'And you did pause,' Aldous adds.

'It was for effect!' Betty exclaims.

Rowena Ghent says, 'It would have been lovely at that length, though.'

'I like short toasts actually,' Thandi says. 'Some people go on and on. Life's short, you know.'

'And death's about the same length,' Owen says.

'Was that a joke?' Liz asks him.

'It was,' Owen says.

'Hmm,' Liz says after a moment's reflection, 'not bad.'

Owen winks at Liz. 'If you have to think about a joke that long, it usually means—'

Betty clears her throat very loudly and begins again. 'We've all had to travel a long way to get here.' She pauses, and no one interrupts her this time. She looks down the table at Rowena, Aldous, and Owen on her right, and Liz, Shelly, and Thandi on her left. She looks under the table, where Paco and Sadie have their own plates. Sadie's stomach growls.

'Sorry,' Sadie barks.

'I can't remember what I wanted to say anyway. Let's just eat,' Betty says with a laugh.

Shelly raises her glass. 'Let's toast to laughter,' she says. 'That's what we always used to toast to at our grandfather's house.'

'Oh, that's lovely!' Rowena says. 'To laughter!'

'To laughter and forgetting!' Liz adds with a mischievous grin in Betty's direction.

'To laughter and forgetting!' the table choruses. The other guests raise their glasses. Liz takes a small sip of her wine. She thinks it is bitter and sweet at the same time. She takes another small sip and decides it is actually more sweet than bitter.

After everyone has finished eating and passed into the traditional postmeal coma, Owen offers to help Liz with the dishes.

'You wash, I'll dry,' Liz tells him.

'But washing's the hard part,' Owen protests.

Liz smiles. 'You said you wanted to *help*. You didn't specify *dry*.'

Owen rolls up his left sleeve and then his right one. Liz notices a tattoo on his right forearm. It is a large red heart with the words 'Emily Forever' inside it.

'I didn't know you'd be like that.' His voice has a mischievous lilt.

'Like what?'

'The type of person who'd stick a guy with all the washing,' he says.

Liz watches as he removes his wedding band, placing it carefully on the edge of the sink. She is still getting used to the notion that someone of Owen's age, seventeen, could be married. Of course, on Elsewhere, this is relatively commonplace.

Liz and Owen soon achieve a satisfying rhythm of washing and drying. Owen whistles a tune as he washes. Although Liz is not exactly a fan of whistling, she finds Owen's whistling, if not pleasant, tolerable. She likes the whistler, if not the whistling itself.

Several minutes of whistling later, Owen turns to Liz, 'I'm taking requests.'

'Owen, that's a really nice offer, but the thing is'—Liz pauses—'I don't really like whistling.'

Owen laughs. 'But I've been whistling for like ten minutes. Why didn't you say anything?'

'Well, I was already a person who would stick a person with washing; I didn't want to be a person who would stick a person with washing *and* not let him whistle.'

'Maybe you'd prefer if I hummed?'

'Whistling's fine,' Liz says.

'Hey, I'm just trying to entertain you here.' Owen laughs again. After a second, Liz joins him. Although nothing particularly funny has been said, Liz and Owen find they cannot stop laughing. Liz has to stop drying the dishes and sit down. It has been such a long time since Liz has laughed this hard. She tries to remember the last time.

The week before Liz died, Zooey and she were trying on sweaters at the mall. Studying herself in the dressing room mirror, Liz said to Zooey, 'My breasts look like little tepees.' Zooey, who had even smaller breasts than Liz, retorted, 'If yours are tepees, mine are tepees that the cowboys came and burned down.' For some reason, this observation struck both girls as ridiculously funny. They laughed so long and so loudly that the salesclerk had to come and ask them if they needed help.

That had been in March; now it was November. Has it really been eight months since Liz has laughed that hard?

'What's wrong?' Owen asks.

'I was thinking that it had been a long time since I laughed like that,' Liz says. 'A really long time.' She sighs. 'It was when I was still alive. I was with my best friend, Zooey. It wasn't even anything very funny, you know?'

Owen nods. 'The best laughs are like that.' He washes the last plate and gives it to Liz to dry. He turns off the water and replaces his ring on his finger.

'I guess I'm a little homesick,' Liz admits, 'but it's the worst kind of homesickness because I know I can't ever go back there or see them ever again.'

'That doesn't just happen to people in Elsewhere, Liz,' says Owen. 'Even on Earth, it's difficult to ever go back to the same places or people. You turn away, even for a moment, and when you turn back around, everything's changed.'

Liz nods. 'I try not to think about it, but sometimes it hits me all at once. Whoosh! And I remember I'm dead.'

'You should know that you're doing really well, Liz,' says Owen. 'When I first came to Elsewhere, I was pretty much addicted to the ODs for a whole year.'

'That happened to me, too,' Liz says, 'but I'm better now.'

'It's common actually. It's called Watcher Syndrome, and some people never get over it.' Suddenly, Owen looks at his watch. It is already nine thirty, and the Observation Decks close at ten. 'I'm sorry to be so abrupt,' says Owen, 'but I have to run. I go see my wife, Emily, every Thursday night.'

'I know,' Liz says. 'A while ago, I was sitting next to you at the ODs and I asked you who you were there to see.'

In the back of his mind, Owen vaguely remembers a withered girl with dirty hair and worn pajamas. He looks at the girl with the clear eyes standing before him and wonders if she could possibly be the same person. 'Pajamas?' he asks.

'I was a little sad at the time.'

'You look much better now,' says Owen. 'Thank you for dinner and thank your grandmother for me, too.'

Sadie wanders into the kitchen just as Owen is leaving. She puts her fuzzy golden head onto Liz's lap, indicating that Liz should stroke it.

'No one will ever love me like that,' Liz says to her.

'I love you,' Sadie says.

'I love you, too,' Liz says to Sadie. Liz sighs. The only love she inspires is the canine kind.

Owen reaches the Observation Deck five minutes before it closes. Although she is not supposed to let people into the decks for the last ten minutes before closing, Esther knows Owen and waves him through. 'You're late tonight, Owen,' the attendant remarks.

Owen sits at his usual binoculars, places a single eternim in the slot, and raises his eyes. He finds Emily in what is a fairly typical pose for her. She is sitting in front of her bathroom mirror, brushing her long red hair with a silver brush. Owen watches Emily brush her hair for about thirty seconds more and then he turns away.

I am wasting my death, Owen says to himself. I am like one of those people who spend all their lives watching TV instead of having real relationships. I have been here nearly ten years, and my most significant relationship is still with Emily. And Emily thinks I'm dead. And I *am* dead. This does her no good, and it does me no good either.

As Owen is leaving, he says to Esther, 'What am I even doing here?'

'Beats me,' Esther replies.

On his way back to his car, Owen makes up his mind to call Liz at work next week. It might be a good start to adopt a dog, he thinks.

A Mystery

Why do two people ever fall in love? It's a mystery.

When Owen calls Liz on Tuesday, he gets right to the point. 'Hello, Liz. I was thinking I might adopt a dog,' he says.

'Of course,' Liz says. 'What sort of dog did you have in mind?'

'Well, I hadn't really thought about it. I guess I'd like a dog I could take to work with me.'

'A small dog?'

'Small's fine as long as he's not too small, and I could take him running and hiking and stuff.'

'So, small's fine as long as she's large?' Liz laughs.

'Right, a small, large dog.' Owen laughs, too. 'And preferably a he.'

'Why don't you come down to the DDA?' Liz suggests.

Later that day, Liz introduces Owen to several possible

candidates. For an adoption to take place on Elsewhere, the dog and the human both have to agree on each other. In truth, the decision is usually more the dog's than the human's.

One by one, the dogs approach Owen and sniff him on the hand and the face. Some lick his hand a bit if they find Owen particularly acceptable. Because Owen does not speak Canine, Liz translates for the dogs when they want to ask him questions.

'Can I sleep in his bed, or does he plan on using a dog bed?' a golden retriever named Jen wants to know.

'What's she saying?' Owen asks.

'She wants to know if she can sleep in your bed.'

Owen looks at the golden retriever and scratches her between the ears. 'Gee, I hadn't really thought about it. Couldn't we play it by ear, girl?'

The golden retriever nods. 'Sure, but I really like to watch television from the couch. You wouldn't tell me to get off the couch all the time, would you?'

'She wants to know if she could stay on the couch,' Liz translates.

'Sure,' says Owen, 'I don't see why not.'

'Okay,' says Jen the Golden Retriever after a moment's reflection. She licks Owen's hand three times. 'Tell him I'll go with him.'

'She says she wants to go with you,' Liz tells Owen.

'Isn't that a little quick?' Owen asks. 'I don't want to hurt her feelings, but . . .' Owen lowers his voice. 'I sort of wanted a boy dog, you know.'

Liz shrugs. 'She's already made up her mind. But don't worry, dogs are really good at this.'

'Oh,' says Owen, shocked by how fast it all seems to be moving.

'Besides,' says Liz cheerfully, 'Jen's already licked you on the hand three times. After that, it's a done deal.'

'I hadn't realized that,' Owen replies.

'So I'll just need you to fill out a couple of forms, and we'll make it official,' Liz says.

'Okay, but would you mind asking her if she gets seasick or anything? I'm on the boat a lot for my job,' Owen says.

'I can understand Human, you know. Not all of us can, but I can. I just can't speak it,' Jen says. 'And I love boats and I don't get seasick. Not much at least. Only if it's really, really rough.'

'Jen understands English and she loves boats,' Liz reports.

Jen continues with her instructions. 'Make sure to tell him I like fresh water at least three times a day. I prefer wet kibble to the dry stuff. I like tennis balls, long walks in the park, and Frisbee. Oh, and I can use the toilet, so please leave the bathroom door open. Yay yay yay yay, I'm so excited!' Jen places her paw on Owen's shoulder. 'I can tell you're going to be just great, Owen!'

'What's she saying?' Owen asks.

'She thinks you're going to be great,' Liz wisely summarizes.

After they fill out all the requisite paperwork, Liz walks Owen and Jen to Owen's Jeep. Jen immediately hops into the backseat and lies down.

'Thanks for your help,' says Owen.

'No problem.' Liz smiles. 'What made you decide to get a dog anyway?'

Owen smiles. 'I hadn't really decided for sure until I came down here, and then Jen sort of decided for me.'

Liz nods. 'That's how it was with me and Sadie, too.'

'The thing is,' says Owen, shifting his weight from one foot to the other, 'I sort of wondered if you might like to do the dishes again.'

'The dishes?' Liz asks.

'Right,' Owen says. 'That was my awkward way of asking you over for dinner.'

'Oh, is that what that was? I hadn't realized.' And she really hadn't. Her experience in such matters is rather limited.

'You know, to thank you for Jen. You wouldn't have to do the dishes. Unless you wanted to, of course. I wouldn't stop you.'

'Um,' says Liz.

Sadie calls to Liz from across the parking lot, 'Liz, telephone!'

'I have a call,' Liz apologizes, heading toward her office. After a moment, she stops. 'Give me a ring sometime! I'm always at work!'

Owen watches as Liz runs inside. Her blond ponytail (her hair had only recently grown long enough to wear that way) bounces up and down rhythmically with each of her steps. There is something pleasing and hopeful about that ponytail, he thinks. He waits until she disappears into the building and then he gets into his car and drives away.

On the drive home, Jen hangs her head out the window and lets her golden ears blow in the wind. She barks the whole way home. 'I don't know why I like my head out the window, I just do,' Jen says while they are stopped at a red light. 'I always liked it that way, even when I was a pup. Is that weird? Is it weird to like something and not even know why you like it?' Owen interprets Jen's barking as excitement and, indeed, his interpretation is perfectly correct.

Why do two people ever fall in love? It's a mystery.

A week later, Liz and Sadie find themselves at Owen Welles's smallish apartment. Jen bounds up to greet them.

'Hi, Liz! Hi, Sadie!' says Jen, who is really excited to see them. 'Nice to see you! Owen's a pretty good boy! He lets me sleep in the bed! I'm trying to convince him to move into a bigger place with a yard! He's trying to cook, but I don't think he's very good! Be nice, though! Don't hurt his feelings!'

Owen smiles when he sees Liz and Sadie at the door. 'Dinner's in here. I hope you like pasta.'

Jen's opinion notwithstanding, Owen is not a bad cook. (Who ever said a dog knew much about cooking anyway?) And Liz is very appreciative of his efforts. It is the first time anyone other than someone in her family has cooked for her.

After dinner, Liz offers to do the dishes. 'I'll wash this time,' she says, 'but you don't have to dry. Or whistle.'

Dishes washed, Liz, Owen, Sadie, and Jen go to the park near Owen's house.

'How are you getting along with Jen?' Liz asks.

'She's great.' Owen smiles. 'I can't believe I never had a dog before.'

'You didn't have one on Earth?'

'We couldn't,' he says. 'Emily was allergic. Still is, I assume.'

Liz nods. 'The way you say her name . . .' she says. 'I can't imagine anyone ever saying my name that way.'

169

'Oh, I doubt that,' says Owen.

'It's true.'

'You died too young,' Owen reflects. 'The boys were probably just intimidated by you. Maybe next time around?'

'Maybe,' Liz says doubtfully. 'I've got a lot of plans for that next time.'

'If I had known you, I might have said your name that way,' Owen says.

'Ah,' Liz says, 'but a person is only allowed to say one other person's name that way, and you're already taken. It's a rule, you know.'

Owen nods but doesn't speak.

His silence stirs a strange but not entirely unpleasant feeling in Liz. His silence makes her bold, and she decides to ask Owen for a favor.

'You can say no, if you want,' Liz begins.

'That sounds scary,' Owen says.

Liz laughs. 'Don't worry. It isn't scary, at least I don't think it's scary.'

'And of course, I already know I can say no.'

'So, the thing is, I'm sort of tired of Betty driving me around everywhere, but I need to learn three-point turns and parallel parking before I get my driver's license. I died before–'

'Sure,' Owen says before Liz is even finished. 'No problem.'

'I could ask Betty, but we sort of have a bad history in the car–'

Owen interrupts Liz. 'I said, no problem. It's my pleasure.'

'Oh,' Liz says, 'thank you.'

'I wouldn't mind hearing about that bad history, however,'

Owen says. 'In fact, maybe I should hear about it *before* we start.'

Why do two people ever fall in love? It's a mystery.

Liz and Owen meet every day after work for the next week. She masters three-point turns with relative ease but finds parallel parking more challenging.

'You just have to visualize yourself in the space,' Owen says patiently.

'But it seems impossible,' says Liz. 'How can something whose wheels move forward and backward, suddenly move side to side?'

'It's the angles,' says Owen. 'You need to turn your steering wheel as extremely as possible, and then slowly back in.'

Another week passes and Liz is still no closer to mastering the elusive parallel parking. She has almost given up hope that she ever will and is beginning to feel like a dunce.

'Look, Liz,' says Owen, 'I'm starting to think it's psychological. There's no reason you shouldn't be able to do this. There's something that's stopping you from wanting to parallel park. Maybe we should call it a night?'

That night, Liz contemplates the reason for her ineptitude and decides to call Thandi.

'Well, speak of the dead,' Thandi says.

'I've been working a lot,' Liz replies, 'and Owen Welles has been teaching me how to drive.'

'I bet he has.'

'What's that supposed to mean?' Liz asks.

'When we were at the dog run, Sadie told Paco that you've

been seeing a lot of Mr. Welles.'

Liz looks at Sadie, who is lying on her back so that Liz can rub her belly. 'Traitor,' she whispers. 'He's in love with someone else,' Liz answers Thandi, 'and besides, we're just friends.'

'Uh-huh,' Thandi says.

Liz tells Thandi about her problem with parallel parking, and asks her, an experienced driver of almost eleven months, if she has any suggestions.

'I think you don't want to learn to parallel park, Liz.'

'Of course I want to learn!' she insists. 'It's just hard! It's not like the rest of driving! It's not logical! It involves visualization and leaps of faith and sleight of hand! You've got to be a freaking magician!'

Thandi laughs. 'Maybe you don't want your lessons with Owen to end, if you catch my drift? I mean, if you had only wanted to learn parking and turning, you could have asked me.'

'You? You haven't even been driving a year!'

'Or Betty?' Thandi suggests.

'Come on! You know our history!'

'I think you're falling in love with him,' Thandi teases. 'I think maybe you're already in lo-ove!' She laughs.

And then Liz hangs up. Thandi could be such an incredible know-it-all. Sometimes Liz cannot even believe that Thandi is her best friend.

The next evening, Liz accomplishes parallel parking three times in a row without error.

'I told you you could do it if you put your mind to it,' says Owen. He looks out the window. 'I suppose we're done here,' he adds.

Liz nods.

'Incidentally, what do you think was blocking you?' Owen asks.

'It's a mystery,' Liz answers. She hands him his keys and gets out of the car.

Liz in Love

How do you know you're in love with someone?' Liz asks Curtis Jest during both their lunch breaks.

Curtis raises an eyebrow. 'Are you saying you're in love with someone?'

'It's a friend,' Liz says stiffly.

Curtis smiles. 'Are you saying you're in love with a friend? Are you trying to tell me something, Lizzie?'

Liz's cheeks burn. 'My interests are purely anthropological,' she replies.

'Anthropological, eh?' His eyes dance in what Liz considers an inappropriate manner.

'If you aren't going to be serious, I'm leaving!' She is indignant.

'My, aren't we touchy! What's a little mirth between friends, Lizzie?' As he is getting nowhere with Liz's mood, Curtis relents. 'Oh all right, darling, let's talk about love.'

'So?'

'In my humble opinion, love is when a person believes that he, she, or it can't live without some other he, she, or it. You are a clever girl, and I imagine this is nothing you haven't heard before.'

'But, Curtis,' she protests, 'we're dead! We have to *live* without people all the time, and we don't stop loving them, and they don't stop loving us.'

'I said *believes*. No one actually needs another person or another person's love to survive. Love, Lizzie, is when we have irrationally convinced ourselves that we do.'

'But, Curtis, doesn't it have anything to do with being happy and making each other laugh and having fun times?'

'Oh, Lizzie.' Curtis laughs. 'If only it were so!'

'It's very rude to laugh at a perfectly natural question,' Liz says.

Curtis stops laughing. 'I am sorry,' he says, truly seeming sorry. 'It's just that only someone who has never been in love would ask such a perfectly absurd question. I long ago decided to stay out of love's way, and I have since been a far happier man.'

On the bus back to work, Liz thinks about what Curtis said. In a roundabout way, he answered her real question, Am I in love with Owen? The answer is no. Of course she isn't in love with him. In retrospect she almost feels silly. For one, Owen is in love with his wife. And two, laughing, having fun, and being happy has nothing to do with being in love. Liz feels relieved. She can continue seeing Owen as much as she likes, safe in the belief that she doesn't love him and he doesn't love her. All this love business is trouble, anyhow. Liz decides she is probably too young for romance. She will focus on work and her friends, and that will be the end of that.

Yes, in a way Liz is relieved. But in another way she isn't. In truth, she enjoyed entertaining the notion that Owen might love her, even a little bit.

The night after Liz mastered parallel parking, Owen finds himself with nothing to do. He spent nearly ten years alone and only three weeks with Liz. And yet he cannot remember what he used to do with his nights for the ten years before the three weeks. Owen stalks about his apartment. He does the type of domestic things one does only when one is trying to fill up time: he cleans the space between the oven and refrigerator with a long wooden spoon that isn't long enough to accomplish its goal; he sweeps under his bed; he tries to read *The Brothers Karamazov*, the new translation that he's been trying to read since before he died without ever making it past page sixty-two; he tries to balance an egg on one end by placing a small mound of salt on his kitchen counter (it doesn't work); he carves a boat out of soap; and he throws out all the socks that have lost their partners. All that takes an hour, and then Owen collapses dejectedly on the couch.

'You should call Liz,' Jen the Golden Retriever says to Owen. Unfortunately, Owen still does not speak Canine, so Jen's wisdom is lost on him.

'I bet Liz and Sadie are doing something fun,' says Jen. 'Why don't we go see them?'

Owen does not answer.

'Owen, you should really learn to speak Canine, because I could tell you a thing or two,' Jen barks in exasperation. 'You're in love with Liz, you know! It's perfectly obvious to everyone!' Jen scratches at the front door and howls. 'Look what you've reduced me to!'

'Do you want to go out?' Owen asks her.

'Oh, you think?' Jen says sarcastically. 'Come on, let's go! I'm taking you on a walk.'

Jen runs Owen all the way across town, and before long, they find themselves in front of Liz's house.

Liz, Sadie, and Betty are all outside the house decorating for the holidays. Liz stands on a ladder, stapling Christmas lights to the roof. Sadie barks when she sees Jen and Owen approach.

'Hello, Jen! Hello, Owen!' Sadie says.

Owen smiles sheepishly at Liz. 'It was Jen's idea, coming here. I don't want to bother you guys, or anything.'

'You're no bother, Owen,' Betty says. Betty's fondness for Owen has increased since he taught Liz how to parallel park. Betty has observed that driving lessons truly improved Liz's overall mood. 'Liz, I can finish up. Why don't you go say hello to your friend?'

Liz climbs down from the ladder. 'I was about to take a break anyway,' she says coolly.

'I'm sorry,' he apologizes, 'it was Jen's idea. We should have called first.'

'Thanks again for the lessons,' Liz says in a slightly friendlier tone. 'I'm sorry I was such a slow learner.'

'It was my pleasure,' he says, suddenly stiff and awkward.

'When will you be getting your license?'

'Well, it turns out the Elsewhere DMV is mainly used to take people's licenses away. New ones are only issued on the second and fourth Tuesdays of the month and not at all in December. I have to wait until January.'

Owen nods. 'Good luck with that.' He twists his wedding band around his finger, a nervous tic of his that Liz finds annoying.

'I should get back to helping Betty with the lights,' Liz says. 'Maybe you'll stop by my house again someday.' Liz smiles and walks away.

Owen calls after her, 'Maybe I'll stop by your house *every* day!'

Liz turns and looks Owen in the eye. 'But I think my parallel parking's up to snuff, don't you?'

'We didn't really cover how to parallel park if you're on a hill. I doubt it'll come up, but—'

'No,' Liz interrupts, 'it's better to be totally safe where parallel parking is concerned.'

'That's what I've always thought,' Owen says.

For Christmas, Liz gives Owen a book called *How to Speak Canine*. Owen gives Liz a pair of fuzzy dice to hang from her rearview mirror. (Or rather, her grandmother's rearview mirror, as Betty's is still the only car Liz drives other than Owen's.)

For the weeks leading up to Liz's driver's license test, Owen and Liz practice parallel parking on all sorts of surfaces. They parallel park on dirt roads, by rivers, under bridges, on the highway, near stadiums, at the beach, and yes, on hills. As test day approaches, Liz finds herself almost hoping she might fail.

On the night before the test, Owen grabs Liz's hand as she is leaving the car.

'Liz, I like you very much,' he says.

'Oh,' she says, 'I like you very much, too!'

Owen is not sure if she means "O" for Owen, or just plain "Oh." He is not sure what difference it would make in either case. He feels the need to clarify. 'When I said "I like you very much," I actually meant "I love you."'

'O,' she says, 'I actually meant the same thing.' She closes the car door behind her.

'Well,' he says to himself, driving back to his apartment, 'isn't that something?'

The next morning, Liz arrives at the Elsewhere DMV at seven o'clock, the first appointment of the day. She passes easily. The test administrator comments that Liz's parallel parking ranks among the "smoothest I have ever seen."

'Congratulations,' Owen says to Liz that night, 'but you know, there's one place we haven't practiced parking yet. You may have your license, but I won't feel totally safe until we've done it.'

'Really? Where?' Liz asks.

'Be patient. You are my driving protégée, and I can't, in good conscience, release you into the world until we've done this last thing.'

'All right.' Liz shrugs. 'Do you care to tell me where this driving rite of passage will take place?'

'No,' Owen replies with a smile, 'I do not.'

So Owen and Liz get into Owen's car yet another time. Liz drives, and Owen gives an occasional direction. He finally tells her to stop in front of a red neon drive-in movie sign.

'Are we going to the movies?' Liz asks, looking up at the enormous movie screen.

'No,' Owen says, as he pays the attendant, 'we are practicing your driving.'

'I think you're taking me to the movies,' Liz insists. 'I think you're taking me on a date.'

'Well, you see things your way, and I see things mine.' Owen laughs.

'Incidentally, what movie are we going to see while I *practice my driving*?' Liz asks.

'It's a remake of some love story. Natalie Wood's the girl, and River Phoenix plays the boy.'

'Sounds good,' Liz comments, 'but I hate remakes.'

'Luckily, you aren't here to see the movie.'

After a quick stop to get popcorn and soda, Liz parks in the front row of cars. They eat their popcorn and wait for the movie to start. 'I think it's strange,' Liz says to Owen, 'that you never call a thing by its name.'

'What do you mean?'

'Well, when you invited me to dinner, you called it "doing dishes." And now you've done the nice thing of taking me to the movies and you call it "practicing my driving." '

'I'm sorry,' Owen says.

'Oh, I'm not angry. I like it actually,' Liz replies. 'It's as if you're speaking in code. It gives me something to do. I've always got to decipher you.'

'I'll try to speak more plainly from now on,' Owen says.

As the movie starts, Owen whispers to Liz, 'I thought maybe now that you've got your license, I might never see you again.'

Liz rolls her eyes. 'You're so stupid sometimes, Owen.'

A week later, Owen and Liz find themselves at the drive-in again.

And a week later, again.

And a week later, again.

'Do you think it's odd that in all the time we've spent in cars we've never made it to the backseat?' Liz asks.

'Now who's speaking in code?' Owen replies.

'Answer the question. Do you think it's odd?'

'It's not that I don't feel anything for you, Liz, because I do.' Owen pauses. 'I'm just not sure it would be right.'

'Why?'

'I'm older than you, for one.'

'Only two years,' she says.

'Only two years and a lifetime or so. But it's not just that I'm older than you.' Owen takes a deep breath. 'I've been here before. And the truth is, intimacy doesn't have all that much to do with backseats of cars. Real intimacy is brushing your teeth together.'

Owen takes off his jacket. Liz looks at his "Emily Forever" tattoo, which for some reason makes her realize that a long time ago, Owen had sex with Emily. Suddenly, Liz notices that the tattoo seems to be brighter and more vivid than ever before. It almost looks like it's glowing.

'Owen,' Liz asks, 'what's with the tattoo?'

'Oh, I got it when I was sixteen, back on Earth. It was stupid really.'

'No, I mean why is it so bright?'

Owen looks down at his arm. 'I know. It's odd, isn't it? I used to think it would fade and go away, but it's only gotten brighter and brighter.'

'You could tattoo my name on your arm, if you want,' Liz adds.

'I could, but tattoos don't really work in Elsewhere. They're gone almost as soon as you put them on,' Owen replies. 'It's not worth all the pain.'

'Don't you understand? It's the *gesture*,' Liz jokes.

'If I'm to understand you correctly, you would have me endure hours of pain and suffering for a gesture?'

'Yes,' Liz deadpans, 'I want to see "Liz For Now" tattooed on your ass.'

'On my ass?'

'Yes, on your ass. It's only nine letters total. It shouldn't hurt too, too much.'

'You're a sadist,' Owen says.

'I thought I was being very kind, actually. I wasn't even going to make you write "Elizabeth." '

'How generous,' he says.

Liz takes Owen's arm in her hands and studies the Emily tattoo up close. Liz thinks, He once loved someone enough to tattoo her name on his arm.

'It wasn't a big deal,' Owen says. 'I was young and stupid.'

'Did it really hurt so much?' Liz asks.

Owen nods.

Liz takes the tattooed arm and presses it to her lips. She kisses the arm and then she bites it.

'Ow,' Owen says.

So this is love, Liz thinks.

Arrivals

If we were to read the book of Thandi, it would tell of a long-forgotten spelling bee (forgotten by everyone but Thandi, that is) where a little girl spells e-c-h-o and at the last crucial moment adds another e to the end; and it would tell of Thandi's first love, an overweight boy named Slim who began dating Thandi's second cousin Beneatha the week after Thandi's funeral; and it would tell of the way a bullet in the head changes everything, how long after it heals, colors look different and smells smell different and even memories are different; and it would tell of a father she never knew, a father who now lives in Elsewhere, a father whom Thandi has no desire to see. But because this is not Thandi's story, we join her on a rather unremarkable day. For her, at least.

At the station where she works, Thandi receives her portion of the arrival names each day after lunch, around one o'clock.

She doesn't need to read them until the five o'clock broadcast, so she uses the four extra hours to go over each name's pronunciation. The extra practice is, for the most part, unnecessary. Thandi rarely makes a mistake; she has a natural ability for pronouncing even the most foreign names. And yet, on this particular day, Thandi stumbles over a simple, phonetic, easily pronounceable name and decides to call Liz about it.

'The name of that woman Owen was married to on Earth? What was it again? Ellen something?' Thandi hopes she misremembered the name.

'Emily Welles.' Liz knows the name as well as she knows her own. 'Why?'

'Emily Welles. That must be a pretty common name.'

'Thandi, what are you getting at?' asks Liz.

'No point in beating around the bush, Liz. Her name was on today's arrivals list. She'll be here on tomorrow's boat.'

Liz's heart beats very quickly, and she can't speak.

'It doesn't necessarily mean anything,' Thandi says.

'No, I know. Of course not. You're right.' Liz takes a deep breath. 'I wonder if Owen knows. He hasn't watched the broadcasts for years.'

Liz decides to meet Owen in person. It is difficult to see him during the day because of all the time he is out to sea. He sometimes docks for lunch, though, so around two, she takes a chance and waits for him at the wharf.

Owen smiles when he sees Liz.

'Now this is a surprise,' he says, embracing her.

Liz had intended to tell Owen about Emily right away, but she can't quite bring herself to do it.

'Is everything all right?' he asks.

Liz nods but doesn't say anything for a while. She just stares out at the water. 'I was just wondering if there are Elsewheres elsewhere,' she says finally. 'It seems strange never to have thought about it before, but does everyone everywhere come to the same place? There must be other boats, right? And maybe they go different places?'

Owen shakes his head. 'We all end up Elsewhere eventually.'

'I only meant, it seems sort of small. Everybody couldn't possibly fit here, could they?'

'Elsewhere is actually very large; it only depends on your perspective.' He takes Liz's hand and flips it over so her palm faces up. 'It's an island really,' he says. With his finger, he lightly draws a map of Elsewhere on her hand. 'This is where the boats come in,' he says, 'and over here is the River back to Earth. I don't know if you know this, but the River is actually in the middle of the ocean. The ocean only parts once a day to allow the babies back to Earth.' Owen draws the squiggly line of the River over the blue veins in Liz's wrist. He traces over to where her thumb is. 'And this is the Well, where we first met.'

Liz stares at her palm. She can still feel where Owen had drawn the invisible borders. Suddenly, she closes her palm and the whole world is erased.

'Emily is coming here,' Liz says.

'She's dead?' Owen says this in a measured, solemn tone.

'Thandi saw her name on the arrivals list. She'll be here tomorrow.'

Owen shakes his head. 'I can't believe it.'

'So what are you going to do?' Liz asks, her voice practically a whisper.

'I'm going to meet her at the pier,' Owen replies.

'After that?'

'I'm going to take her to my house.'

'So you think she'll probably stay with you, then?'

'Liz, of course she'll stay with me.'

'What about us?' Liz whispers.

Owen doesn't answer her for the longest time. Finally, he says, 'I do love you, but I met her first.' He places his hand on top of hers. 'I'm not sure what to do, what's right.'

Liz looks at Owen. He seems truly miserable, and Liz doesn't want to be the cause of that misery. She removes her hand from under his. When she speaks, it is in a strong, very adult voice. 'The truth is, Owen,' Liz says, 'we've only just met. You have a responsibility to your wife.' Liz waits to see what Owen will say.

'I don't want to lose our friendship,' he says.

'We'll still be friends,' Liz says. She's disappointed he came around to her reasoning that quickly.

'Oh, Liz, you're the best!' Owen embraces her again. 'Emily's a great girl. I think you'll really like her.'

Later that night, curled up in bed next to Sadie, Liz wonders how someone could claim to love a person one minute and not love her the next.

Of course, Liz is rather inexperienced in such matters. As many have discovered, it is entirely possible (though not particularly desirable) to love two people with all your heart. It is entirely possible to long for two lives, to feel that one life can't come close to containing it all.

The ship arrives at sunset. Owen wonders if Emily will recognize him. After all, it has been nearly ten years since they last saw each other. He notices that other people on the pier are carrying handmade cardboard signs with people's names written on them. Maybe he should have made one of those, too?

Emily is the second person off the ship. Even from five hundred yards away, the distance from Owen's position on the pier to the ship's gangplank, Owen can tell that it is her. The sight of her distinctive red hair makes Owen want to sing. She must be thirty-six now, but to him, she looks exactly the same as when he died.

Upon spotting Owen, Emily smiles and waves. 'Owen,' she calls.

'Emily!' Owen pushes through the crowd.

As soon as they reach each other, Owen and Emily embrace and kiss. It feels like a movie to Owen. He has waited so long for her, and now she is here.

'Did you miss me?' Emily asks.

'Oh, just a little,' he says.

Emily holds Owen at arm's length, looking him up and down. 'You look good,' she pronounces.

'You don't look so bad yourself,' Owen says.

Emily pushes Owen's hair back behind his ears. 'You look young,' she says, furrowing her brow. She looks around the pier. 'Are we all young here?'

'Eventually, yes,' Owen replies.

'What do you mean "eventually"?' Emily asks.

Owen smiles. 'Don't worry,' he says, 'it all works out in the end. I'll explain everything.' Owen takes Emily's hand. As he leads her out to the parking lot, he feels that the sad times are behind him, once and for all.

In the car, Emily asks, 'So how does this work? Do I stay with you?'

'Of course you do,' Owen answers. 'You're my wife.'

'Am I? Still?'

'Of course you are.' Owen laughs. 'Who else would you be?'

'But what about "till death do us part" and all of that?' she asks.

'I've always thought of us as married,' Owen says, 'and now we aren't parted anymore.'

Emily nods but doesn't say anything.

'Haven't *you* always thought of us as married?' Owen asks.

'In a way, I suppose I have,' Emily says. 'Yes.'

'Have I told you how happy I am to see you?' Owen asks.

That night in bed, Owen says to Emily, 'Is it wrong that I *love* the flu? Is it wrong that I want to sing songs in praise of the flu?'

'I'm glad my death brings out the troubadour in you. But I am dead here, you know. A little gravity is in order.' Emily laughs and says, 'The flu. What an entirely stupid way for me to go.' And then she sneezes. 'Hey, I thought there wasn't any sickness here,' she says.

'There isn't,' Owen says.

And then she sneezes again. And Owen remembers that she is allergic to dogs. (He had decided to leave Jen with Liz for

189

Emily's first night in town—he had suspected that he and Emily might want to be alone.) 'The thing is . . .' Owen begins. 'Well, I have this dog. I know you used to be allergic, but–'

Emily interrupts him. 'Maybe I'm not allergic anymore? I mean, maybe I'm not allergic here.'

Owen is doubtful. 'Maybe.'

'Maybe I'm just sneezing because I'm still recovering from the flu. Is that even possible?'

Owen doesn't think this is possible, but he chooses not to say so. 'Maybe.'

The next day, while Emily is at her acclimation appointment, Owen brings Jen back home. Even though Jen's loyalties are with Liz, Jen is also a pragmatist. She knows it is important to make a good first impression with Emily. In her experience, very few people can resist a wagging tail, and the moment Emily walks through the door, Jen begins wagging her tail furiously. 'Hello, Emily. I'm Owen's dog, Jen. Pleased to meet you.'

'Hello, Jen,' Emily says.

Jen holds out a paw for Emily to shake, and Emily sneezes on it.

'Gross,' Jen says and then thinks better of it. 'Gesundheit.'

'Thank you,' Emily says. And then, 'Owen, is it strange that your dog is talking?'

'Terrific, Emily, you understand Canine!' Owen says. 'I don't myself, but I wish I did. Some people are naturals, like'—he pauses—'my friend Liz.'

Emily sneezes again.

'Are you allergic to dogs?' Jen asks.

'I used to be, on Earth,' Emily concedes, 'but I don't think I am here, right?'

Jen looks doubtful.

Emily continues, 'I probably just think I'm allergic because I was before. Maybe it's psychosomatic?' Emily sneezes.

'What's "psychosomatic"?' Jen asks worriedly.

'It means, it's all in my head. So eventually, I'll stop being allergic to you, I'm sure.'

'Do you think?' Jen cocks her head.

'Um, maybe.' Emily sneezes again. 'Let's hope so.'

But the next morning, Emily's eyes are swollen and red, and she is sneezing and coughing nonstop. Despite her allergies, Emily still acts as translator between Jen and Owen.

'Look, Owen,' Jen says, 'I don't want to live with a person who's constantly sneezing when I'm around.' She lowers her tail pathetically. 'It makes me feel unwelcome.'

'I really am sorry about my allergies,' Emily says to Jen. Then she tells Owen, 'Jen says she doesn't want to live with me because my sneezing is making her uncomfortable.'

'Okay,' Owen says. He is glad that Jen made this suggestion before he had to.

'Owen, aren't you going to protest at least a little?' Jen lowers her ears now. 'I mean, I was living here first. Maybe *she* could live somewhere else?'

'She suggests that I could live somewhere else, as she was living here first. Owen, maybe she has a point?' Emily sneezes.

'No,' Owen says. 'You're my wife. And we'll figure something out.'

That night, Jen, who is not an outdoor dog, sleeps on the porch. 'We'll figure something out,' Owen repeats, trying to soothe Jen.

'Can't I at least stay on the couch?' Jen whines. 'You promised I could always stay on the couch when we first met.' Unfortunately, Owen doesn't understand a word she is saying.

Three days later, Owen leaves Jen at Liz's house. Emily still believes her allergies are only temporary, but Jen is tired of sleeping outside.

'How's it going?' Liz asks Owen. She thinks he looks tired but happy.

'Great,' he says. And then he whispers, 'I hope I can get Jen back in a couple days, but it's all a little much for Emily.'

'Of course.' Liz smiles tightly.

'How's your driving coming?' Owen asks. 'Parallel parking giving you any trouble, because I could–'

She interrupts him. 'No.'

'Thank you for taking Jen.'

'It's nothing.' Liz shrugs. 'Sometimes these things just don't work out.'

Owen starts to walk away.

'By the way,' Liz asks, 'what did Emily die of?'

'The flu.'

'But I thought she was a doctor! She must have had a vaccination.'

'She did. It didn't work. It's not always a sure thing, you know.'

'I do,' Liz replies.

Watching Owen drive away, Liz thinks about the flu. She thinks how everyone else she knows died of much more respectable causes: Aldous and wife (plane crash), Betty (breast cancer), herself and Sadie (hit by cars), Curtis and Thandi's cousin Shelly (drug overdoses), Thandi (gunshot wound to the head), Owen (fire), Esther (Alzheimer's/related causes), Paco (drowning). Now, those were deaths, Liz thinks. Who the hell dies of the flu except really old people? Liz thinks how everything is changing, all because stupid Emily couldn't be bothered to wash her hands properly.

When Owen returns, Emily is reading a photocopied pamphlet with the title 'Elsewhere Office of Avocation Services Guide to Alternative Professions.' She says, 'It appears I can't be a doctor anymore. I could work at a healing center I suppose, but that's more like nursing.'

'I'm sorry,' Owen says.

'Don't apologize. Even if I could still be a doctor, I'm not sure that I would want to be one anyway.'

'Do you know what you want to do instead?' he asks.

'Maybe I'd like to be one of those people who catch Earth people reading from the ODs and then transcribe the Earth books for here.'

'You can't mean a keeper of books?'

'That's exactly what I mean. You have to be good with punctuation, which I am, and a good listener, which I also am, and like to stay up late at night when people do most of their reading, which I also like.'

'Sounds sort of boring though,' Owen says.

Emily shrugs. 'I never had any time to read for pleasure when I was a doctor. And besides, it's just something to do; it's not my whole life.'

Owen just shakes his head. 'You were always so ambitious. A keeper of books? That just doesn't sound like you.'

'Maybe I'm different now,' Emily says.

Owen decides to change the subject. 'How are your parents?'

'Good,' Emily says.

'And your sister?'

'Allie's divorcing Joe,' Emily says.

Owen says, 'They were so in love.'

'Not for a long time, O.'

'I still can't believe it,' Owen says.

'You haven't seen them for a while,' Emily says. 'You missed some things.'

'Okay,' Owen says, 'tell me everything about the last ten years in thirty seconds, go!'

'Um,' she says, 'I . . .'

'Faster,' he says, looking at his watch, 'you've only got twenty-five, twenty-four seconds left.'

Emily laughs. She tries to speak as quickly as she can. 'Finished medical school. Went into burns in your honor. Being a doctor was okay. Sickness, accidents, death. I spent a lot of time with my sister . . .'

'Ten seconds left.'

'Oh God, I've really got to hurry then. Allie had a baby, a boy, and she named it Owen. I was a good aunt.' And then her voice changes, 'Did you know when you died I was pregnant? We had a baby; I lost it, O.'

'Time,' Owen calls out halfheartedly. 'I didn't know.'

'What happens to babies when they die before they're

born?' Emily asks.

'I think they don't make it all the way down the River to start with. They just float back and gather their strength until they can start swimming again. I'm not sure exactly.'

'So the baby becomes another baby? Someone else's baby?'

'Something like that,' Owen agrees.

'Oh, I wish I'd known that before. It wouldn't have seemed so sad.'

'I wish I could have helped you,' he says.

Emily sighs.

'We had a baby,' Owen repeats. 'Why didn't I know?'

'Because I didn't know myself until after you died. I lost it in the second month, and I wasn't really showing that much.'

'But I still should have known! All I did was watch you!'

'Some things we can't see. Some things we don't want to see,' she says.

'And I thought you were just sad over me,' he whispers.

'There was certainly that, too.'

'I would have liked to have met that baby,' Owen says. 'Did you name it?'

Emily nods. 'I did.'

'What was the name?'

Emily whispers the name in Owen's ear.

'I like that,' he says softly. 'Not too fancy, not too plain. I think he would have liked it, too.'

At night, Emily starts sleeping on the sofa while Owen stays in the bedroom. They keep different hours and quickly find it to be easier this way. Besides, he feels happy just knowing she is across the wall from him. It reminds him of when they were kids growing up in New York, and they used to knock Morse code to each other.

Every day with Emily is like a small miracle to him. There she is in his chair. And there she is wearing his shirt. And there she is doing the dishes. And there she is sleeping. And she's everywhere. He can't believe how everywhere she is. He wants to bite her just to make sure she's real. He wants to take pictures of her just because he can. And when he's supposed to be doing other things, he just sits there and stares at her. And Emily's so amazing. She wants to see things, so he takes her to all his favorite places in Elsewhere. And she asks a lot of questions. (He had forgotten that about her.) And Owen tries his best to answer them, but she's always been smarter than him (now even more so), so he's not sure if all his answers are even satisfactory to her.

Okay, a couple of things do annoy him a little bit. He is ashamed to even mention them. She's messy. And she likes to start home improvement projects, but she never actually finishes them. And she stays up late and is noisy even when she's trying to be quiet. And she never takes her hair out of the drain. And she really does ask a lot of questions. And sometimes they run out of stuff to talk about, because all they have in common is the past. So a lot of their conversations begin, 'Do you remember that time . . . ?' And the thing that bothers him most has nothing to do with her.

But Owen tries to ignore these things. This is Emily, after all.

One Saturday afternoon, Liz stops by Owen's house to pick up

Jen's favorite ball. Jen has been bothering Liz to do it for a week, but Liz has been avoiding the task for one reason or another. When Liz finally does go, Owen isn't there, but Emily is. Liz wonders if Emily even knows who she is.

'I'm Liz,' she says stiffly. 'I'm the one watching Jen. You must be Emily.'

'Oh, Liz, it's so nice to meet you.' Emily shakes her hand. 'Thank you for taking care of Jen,' she says. 'I hope I won't be allergic forever and that eventually she'll want to come back.'

Liz nods. 'I'm just here to get Jen's ball and then I'll go.'

'Sure, I'll go get it.' Emily returns with the ball. She looks at Liz. Liz reminds Emily of someone, but she can't quite place who it is. 'How do you know Owen anyway?' Emily asks.

'I . . .' She pauses. 'I helped him adopt Jen. I work for the Department of Domestic Animals. I guess we sort of got to be friends through Jen.'

'That makes sense,' Emily says. 'Can I get you a soda or something? It's just that I haven't met any of Owen's friends, and I'm sort of curious.'

'I really have to go,' Liz says. 'I'm sorry.'

'Oh, all right. Some other time, then?'

Liz nods. She gets into her car as quickly as she can and drives away.

'Hey, Liz,' Emily calls after her, 'you forgot to take Jen's toy!'

At home in bed, Liz cries into her pillow. Betty tries to comfort her.

'Don't cry, doll. There are other fish in the sea,' Betty says.

'I'm not getting any older, if you haven't noticed,' Liz says miserably. 'There's no time for me to find other fish. Who even likes fish? I hate fish!'

'Well, you can still be friends with Owen, can't you?'

Liz says nothing.

'We should really invite them over for dinner,' Betty says.

'Who?'

'Owen and his wife, of course.'

'Why?'

'Because it's nice, and he's your good friend.'

'I think that's a rotten idea,' Liz says.

'Let's invite them for next Saturday,' Betty says. 'I'm really curious about her.'

'I met her today,' Liz says.

'Really? What is she like?'

'She's very pretty,' Liz concedes, 'and very adult.'

Liz gets out of bed and looks in the mirror over her bureau. She wonders if she is already starting to look younger.

About a week later, Emily and Owen come to Betty's house for dinner. Owen is happy to see Jen and proud to introduce Emily to everyone. Betty and Emily spend most of the evening talking to each other. Their conversation is punctuated by Emily's sneezes, even though the dogs had been banished to Liz's room for the occasion. Liz is mostly silent. Owen keeps trying to make eye contact with her, but she consciously avoids his gaze. On account of Emily's allergies and Liz's sullenness, the evening ends quickly.

After Owen and Emily have left, Betty says, 'Now don't you feel better having done that?'

'Not really,' Liz says.

'She was nice,' Betty adds.

'I didn't say she wasn't,' Liz says through gritted teeth.

In the car on the way home, Emily says to Owen, 'You like Liz, don't you?'

Owen doesn't answer.

'You don't have to feel bad about it,' Emily continues. 'It would be the most natural thing in the world if you did. She's your age, and you couldn't have known I would be coming here.'

Owen shakes his head. 'I love you, Em. I'll always love you.'

'I know you do,' Emily says.

That same night, Liz is about to jump into bed when she notices a large yellow puddle.

'What happened in here?' Liz asks Sadie.

'Don't look at me! It was Jen,' Sadie answers. 'I think she's having abandonment issues. She thought Owen was coming to get her tonight.'

'That's it!' Liz yells. 'I'm driving over there!' She grabs Betty's keys from the counter and slams the door.

With her pulse racing, Liz rings Owen's doorbell.

'Are you ever planning to come and get Jen?' Liz yells. 'Or are you just planning to leave her with me for the rest of your life?'

'Owen, who's at the door?' Emily calls.

'It's only Liz,' Owen yells back.

'Hi, Liz,' Emily calls out.

' "Only Liz"?' Liz is indignant.

Owen closes the door behind him and leads Liz off the

porch. 'You don't say a word to me all night, and then you come over here to yell at me!'

'Owen,' Liz says, 'I don't think it's fair what you're doing to Jen. She feels abandoned and upset.'

'Oh, come on, I'm sure she's fine living with you. Jen loves you,' Owen says.

'Jen may love me, but I am not her owner. She peed on my bed. Dogs who are housebroken only pee on people's beds when they're having issues.'

'Well,' Owen says, 'I'm sorry about that.'

'So when are you planning to come and get her?' Liz demands.

'Soon, soon, just as soon as Emily's settled in.'

'It's been two weeks. Don't you think she's settled in enough?'

'You know Emily's allergic.' Owen sighs. 'I don't know what to do.'

'You made a commitment to Jen. You said you would take care of her,' Liz says.

'But I made a commitment to Emily long before I ever met Jen.'

'Oh, for crying out loud! I am so tired of Emily!' Liz yells.

'And I think this isn't about Jen at all!' Owen yells back.

'For your information, I don't want anything to do with you. I wouldn't even be here if you hadn't left your dog with me!'

'Oh yeah?' says Owen.

'Yeah.'

And then, because there is nothing left to say, they kiss. Liz wasn't sure if Owen had kissed her or if she had, in fact, kissed him. Either way, it's not quite how she imagined their first kiss would be.

When Liz finally pulls away from Owen, she sees Emily staring back at her. Emily doesn't look angry exactly, just sort of curious.

'Hello,' Emily says. 'I heard yelling.' She smiles a very strange smile. 'I guess I'll leave you two alone,' she says, not unkindly.

'Emily–' Owen says. But Emily is already gone. 'This is all your fault!' Owen yells at Liz.

'My fault? But you kissed me.'

'I mean, you being here. You existing. You're making my life so much harder,' Owen says.

'What do you mean?' Liz asks.

'I loved Emily. I *love* her,' Owen says, 'and maybe if I had met you first, things would be different. But this is the way things are.'

Owen sinks onto the porch steps. He looks deflated. 'She's my wife, Liz. There's nothing I can do. Even if I wanted to do something, there's nothing I can do.'

'I'll keep watching Jen,' Liz says before she leaves.

The Sneaker Clause

One night after work, Aldous Ghent stops by the DDA. Liz is one of Aldous's favorite advisees, and he often leaves business with her until the day's end. That evening, he finds Liz, Sadie, and Jen cooped up in Liz's office. It had rained all day, and all three are in particularly black moods. In an argument over whose water bowl was whose, Sadie had bitten Jen's back leg. Though it wasn't a bad bite, Jen's pride is wounded and now she isn't speaking to Sadie.

'Hello, ladies,' Aldous says cheerily. Luckily, Aldous is the type of man who is oblivious to most people's black moods, as he is almost always in a good mood himself. 'Jen, Sadie, I need to speak to Liz alone for a moment.' Both dogs reluctantly get to their feet. Jen affects an inconsistent limp.

'How's Owen?' Aldous asks Liz with a knowing smile.

'I wouldn't know,' Liz replies.

'What's Shakespeare say? "The course of true love never did run smooth," ' Aldous teases her.

'I wouldn't know,' Liz repeats.

'If I recall, it's from *A Midsummer Night's Dream*.'

'We had only gotten up to *Macbeth* in English, then I died.'

'Well, Elizabeth, we do have Shakespeare here, you know.'

'The thing about Shakespeare is you can only read him if someone is making you,' Liz says. 'On Elsewhere, no one makes you read Shakespeare or anything else.' Liz sighs. 'Aldous, what do you want already?'

'I'm sure you'll find that whatever quarrel you and Owen have had will quickly mend itself,' Aldous says.

'I doubt that,' Liz says. 'Owen's wife has arrived from Earth.'

'My, that is a bump,' says Aldous, momentarily fazed by Liz's revelation. And then the ever-present smile returns to his face. 'When you've lived as long as I have, you'll find that the world has a way of working things out,' Aldous says.

'Whatever that means,' Liz says under her breath.

'I've come to remind you that next week marks the one-year anniversary of your arrival in Elsewhere,' Aldous says. 'So, congratulations, Elizabeth!'

'Is that all?' says Liz. Aldous always takes a ridiculously long time to get to the point. Normally she finds him amusing, but today she wants to scream.

'Well, it's just a formality really, but I need to make sure you don't want to exercise the Sneaker Clause.'

'What was that again?'

'A Sneaker is a teenager or younger person who returns to Earth before his or her proper passage,' says Aldous. 'If you recall, you had one year to decide, and your year is just about finished.'

Liz considers what Aldous is saying. Somehow this whole experience with Owen and Emily has made her feel entirely exhausted and pessimistic. What is the point of loving anyone? To Liz, all the effort of working, living, loving, talking has begun to seem just that: effort. In fifteen years (less, actually), she would just forget everything anyway. All things considered, it is beginning to seem preferable to speed the process up a bit. 'So I can still go?' Liz asks.

'You're not saying you want to go?' asks Aldous.

Liz nods.

Aldous looks at Liz. 'Well, I must say I'm surprised, Elizabeth. I'd never pegged you for a Sneaker.' Aldous's eyes tear. 'And I thought you had such a successful acclimation.'

'What would I have to do?' Liz asks.

'Inform your friends and loved ones of your decision. By letter or in person, it's your choice. Perhaps you should speak to Betty about this, Elizabeth.'

'This is what I want, Aldous,' Liz says. 'Wait, you won't tell her, will you?'

Aldous shakes his head, looking uncharacteristically tortured. 'Everything we discuss is always confidential. I couldn't tell her, even if I wanted to. Even though I probably should.'

Now Aldous begins to cry outright. 'Was it something I did? Or didn't do?' he asks. 'Please don't spare my feelings.'

'No, I think it was just me,' Liz comforts him as best she can.

It is determined that Liz's Release will take place Sunday morning, the one-year anniversary of her arrival on Elsewhere and the last possible day she could exercise the clause. She will leave with all the babies on the River. It will be strange, Liz thinks, to be among so many babies. Furthermore, Liz will have to be wrapped in swaddling clothes, which would be totally humiliating if anyone saw her. Of course, no one will see her anyway.

The only person Liz decides to tell is Curtis Jest. The obvious choices—Betty, Thandi, or Sadie—would try to talk her out of it, and Liz isn't in the mood for any more drama. She isn't speaking to Owen. So basically that leaves Curtis. He always seems amused by other people's lives, but decidedly detached and apathetic. He would be sad to see her go, but he wouldn't do anything to try to stop her. And that is exactly what Liz wants.

Still, Liz waits as long as possible to talk to Curtis. She tells him on the Saturday night before she is set to leave.

'So I suppose there's no talking you out of this?' Curtis says, as the two of them sit on the wharf, their legs dangling over the side.

'Nope,' Liz replies, 'it's decided.'

'And this isn't because of Owen?'

Liz sighs. 'No,' she says finally, 'not really. But maybe I just wish I could have what he has.'

'I don't follow, Lizzie.'

'The thing is, Owen had Emily from before, from Earth. I have nothing from before on Earth. Emily was Owen's first love, and I want that, I want to be someone's first. Can you understand that? It sometimes feels that in this backward life, nothing that happens to me is ever new. Everything that happens has happened to someone else before. I feel like I'm getting everything secondhand.'

'Liz,' Curtis says seriously, 'I think you would find that even if you were still on Earth, living a forward life, everything that happened to you would still have happened to someone else.'

'Yes,' Liz concedes, 'but it wouldn't be so predetermined. I wouldn't know when I was going to die. I wouldn't know that in less than fifteen years, I would be a stupid baby again. I would get to be an adult. I would have a life of my own.'

'You have a life of your own.'

Liz shrugs. She feels no need to have this conversation.

'Liz, I must tell you, I think you're making a grave mistake.'

Suddenly, Liz turns on him. 'You're a fine one to talk! Look at you, you sit on this wharf all day, day after day, and you do nothing! You see no one! You don't sing! You're half dead, really!'

'I'm all dead, actually,' Curtis jokes.

'Everything is a joke to you; everything is amusing. Well, why aren't you singing? Why don't you sing something, Curtis?'

'Because I have already done that once,' Curtis says firmly.

'So you don't miss it at all? You can't honestly expect me to believe that you're happy just being a fisherman. I mean, I've never even seen you catch anything!'

'I do catch fish; I just throw them all back.'

'That's completely stupid and pointless!'

'Not at all. We direct the fish back to Earth and, furthermore, we keep the wharf picturesque. Fishing is a fine, noble profession,' says Curtis.

'Unless you're supposed to do something else!'

Curtis doesn't answer for a while. 'Last week, I met a gardener named John Lennon.'

'What does that have to do with anything?' Liz asks. She

isn't in the mood for Curtis's bullshit.

'Nothing. It's only to say that just because someone did something before doesn't mean they have to do it still.'

'Do you know what I think?' Liz asks. 'I think you're a coward!' She stands and walks away.

'Takes one to know one, Lizzie my gal!' Curtis calls after her.

Liz stays up all night drafting a letter to Betty.

Dear Betty,

~~Every day is exactly like the day before, and I can't stand it anymore. I feel like I'll never get to the good part. Death is just one big rerun, you know.~~

~~It's not about Owen.~~

~~By now, you probably know I've gone back to Earth~~

Gone back to Earth as Sneaker.

Please don't worry.

~~I'm sorry it has to be this way.~~

I'm sorry.

Take care of Sadie and Jen for me.

Love,

Liz

Omitting the crossed-out parts, Liz rewrites the letter on a fresh sheet of paper and goes to sleep.

Late that night, Owen hears a knocking on the wall. He listens to the knocks, which seem to have a familiar, steady rhythm: it is Emily knocking Morse code to him.

'Do you want me to go?' she knocks.

He doesn't answer.

'I want to go,' she knocks.

He doesn't answer.

'Knock twice so I know you've heard me.'

He takes a deep breath and knocks twice.

'This isn't working out,' she knocks.

'I know,' Owen knocks back.

'I will always love you,' she knocks, 'but our timing just isn't right.'

'I know,' Owen knocks.

'I'm a thirty-five-year-old woman; I'm different now,' she knocks.

'I know,' Owen knocks.

'You're seventeen,' she knocks.

'Sixteen,' he knocks.

'Sixteen!' she knocks.

'I'm sorry,' he knocks softly.

'It isn't your fault, O. It's just life,' she knocks.

'But we're dead,' he knocks.

Owen can hear Emily laugh in the other room. No knocks

follow, and then she is standing in his room.

'When you first died, I wanted to die, too. I didn't want to be alive without you,' Emily says. 'You were my whole life. I had no memories that didn't contain you somehow.'

Owen nods.

'But I moved on. I stopped waiting for you. In truth, I didn't believe I would ever see you again,' Emily says.

'You never married,' Owen says.

'I had done that before. And to even consider doing it again, you were the standard against which all others had to be judged.' She laughs. 'The funny thing is, I had actually met someone a couple of months before I died. It wasn't serious, not yet, but it had possibility.'

'I never saw that! I never once saw you with another guy!' Owen says.

'Well, I suspect you hadn't been watching me very closely during that time,' Emily says.

Owen looks away.

'On some level, I could always feel you watching me, Owen, and I noticed when you stopped,' Emily says.

Owen doesn't answer.

'It's all right for you to be in love with someone else. You shouldn't feel guilty,' Emily says gently.

'At first, I think I liked her because she reminded me of you,' he says quietly.

'Or me twenty years ago.'

Owen looks at Emily and for the first time since she'd arrived on Elsewhere, he really sees her. She's pretty, maybe even more so than she was as a girl. But she's different. She's older, more angular. Her eyes are changed, but he can't say just how. 'I don't really know you anymore, do I?' he says sadly.

She kisses him on the forehead, and he wants to cry.

'Some couples work out; some couples make it here,' Owen says. 'Why can't we be those people?'

'I wouldn't worry too much about it,' Emily says. 'And in any case, I'm glad I got to see you again.'

'But it seems unfair, doesn't it? We were supposed to grow old together and all that.'

'Well, that wasn't going to happen anyway. Not here at least,' Emily points out. 'And I think we were luckier than most,' she says. 'We had a great life together, and we got a second chance, too. How many people can say that?'

'Is this because of that night on the porch?' Owen asks.

'Not at all,' Emily assures him. 'But as you mention it, would you like to know what I saw out there?' She pauses. 'I saw two kids in love.'

Owen closes his eyes and when he opens them again, she is gone. He feels a strange ache in his forearm. He examines his tattoo, which is more vivid than he can ever remember it being, even when it had first been applied. The heart throbs and pulses almost like a real heart. And then, in a moment, the tattoo is gone, too. Aside from a slight redness, his skin is bare. It is as if the tattoo had never been there at all.

Right before he falls asleep, he vows to go see Liz first thing in the morning.

To Earth

On the morning of Liz's Release, she wakes at four o'clock. All launches take place at sunrise when the tide exposes the River, and she arrives about fifteen minutes early.

A team of launch nurses prepares the babies to be Released into the River. Liz's nurse is named Dolly.

'My,' says Dolly when she sees Liz, 'we don't often get big girls like you.'

'I'm a Sneaker,' Liz replies.

'Yeah, Joleen normally handles the Sneakers, but she's on vacation. Sneaker or not, you have to take off all your clothes, and then I'll swaddle you up.'

'Can't I at least leave on my underwear?' Liz asks.

'Sorry, everyone's got to wear their birthday suit back to Earth,' Dolly says. 'I know it's probably a little embarrassing at your age, but that's how it works. Most of the babies don't know the difference. Besides, no one'll know you're naked under the swaddling clothes anyway.' Dolly hands Liz a paper gown. 'You can wear this in the meantime.'

Naked but for the gown, Liz lies down on a table with wheels like a hospital gurney. The launch nurse begins to wrap Liz in white linen bandages. She starts with Liz's feet, bandaging Liz's legs together, and works her way up to Liz's head. When she reaches the middle, she removes Liz's paper gown and begins to bind Liz's arms to her sides.

'Why do you have to bind the arms?' Liz asks.

'Oh, it helps the current pull you to Earth if you're more streamlined, and it also keeps the babies warm,' Dolly answers.

Dolly leaves Liz's face open, but the rest of Liz's body is tightly bound. Liz looks like a mummy. She feels terrible wrapped up this way, and she can barely breathe.

Dolly rolls Liz over to the edge of the beach. She lowers her into the water. Liz feels the cool water saturate her bandages.

'What happens to the swaddling clothes when I get to Earth?'

'Don't worry. The cloth will have mostly deteriorated by then, and the River washes away what's left,' says Dolly. 'When the sun starts to rise over the horizon, you'll be able to see the River. I'll give you a push, and the current will carry you all the way to Earth. I am told the journey feels like a week, but you'll probably lose track of time much before then.'

Liz nods. She can make out the beginnings of a reddish light just over the horizon. It will be soon.

'Do you mind if I ask you a question?' Dolly asks Liz.

Liz shakes her head, and it practically causes her whole body to shake because of the tight cloth.

'What makes a person want to go back to Earth early?' Dolly asks.

'What do you mean?' Liz replies.

'I mean, it's all life, isn't it? Why are you in such a rush to get back?'

At that moment, the sun appears in the sky. The ocean splits in two, and the River is revealed.

'Sunrise,' says Dolly. 'Time to go. Well, have a good trip!' Dolly gives Liz a push down the River.

Curtis Jest cannot sleep. He tosses and turns in his wooden cot. Finally, he gives up on sleeping and gets out of bed.

Curtis hitches a ride across town to Liz's house. He knows Liz is living with her grandmother. He decides that he must inform this woman about Liz's decision, even if it means breaking Liz's confidence. For the first time in ages, he laments losing his rock star status. (Rock stars always have fast cars.)

At 6:15 a.m., he rings Betty's doorbell.

'Hello, I'm looking for Lizzie's grandmother,' Curtis says. He stares at Betty. 'Good Lord, you wouldn't be her, would you?'

'Yes, I'm Elizabeth's grandmother. And you are?'

'I'm–' Curtis begins. For a moment, he completely forgets his name and his whole reason for coming. Instead, he considers what color you would call Betty's eyes. Gray-blue, he decides. Gray-blue like a foggy morning, like the water in a stone fountain, like the moon or maybe the stars. Betty with the gray-blue eyes. That might make a good song–

'Yes?' Betty interrupts his reverie.

Curtis clears his throat, lowers his voice, stands up straighter, and resumes speaking. 'I am Curtis Sinclair Jest, formerly of the band Machine. I am a trusted confidant of Elizabeth's, which is why I come to you at this hour. I must tell you something very urgent about Lizzie.'

'What about Liz?' Owen asks, walking up behind Curtis from the driveway. 'I need to talk to her right now.'

Curtis says, 'Lizzie is in trouble, Betty. We'll need your car.'

Betty takes a deep breath. 'What's happened? What's happened to Elizabeth?' She gives up trying to disguise the terror in her voice. 'I want to know what's happened to my granddaughter!' she yells.

Curtis takes Betty's hand. 'She's headed back to Earth, and we've got to stop her.'

'You can't mean she's sneaking?' Owen asks.

Curtis nods.

'But it's already dawn!' Betty exclaims.

The three look up at the jaundiced sky, which grows brighter with every second.

'My car's faster,' Owen says, running back down the driveway.

'God help us,' Betty whispers before following him.

As she is pulled faster and faster toward Earth, Liz begins to think of Elsewhere and of all the people she's met there. She thinks of how those people might feel when they discover she has taken her leave without even telling them.

She thinks of Thandi.

214

She thinks of Betty.

She thinks of Sadie.

She thinks of Paco, of Jen, of all the dogs . . .

And she thinks of Owen.

But mainly she thinks of herself. Continuing down the River will mean, for all practical purposes, the end of Liz. And when she looks at it that way, she suddenly wonders if she hasn't made a colossal mistake.

And then she wonders if it's too late to correct it.

Because it wouldn't be for Owen or for any of them that she would return to Elsewhere. With or without Owen, almost fifteen years was a long time. Almost fifteen years was a gift. Anything could happen here in Elsewhere, the place where Liz's life had supposedly ended.

If I interrupt this life, I will never know how my life was supposed to turn out. A life is a good story, Liz realizes, even a crazy, backward life like hers. To cling to her old forward life was pointless. She would never have her old forward life. This backward life *was* her forward life when she really thought about it. It isn't her time, and her desire to know how the story will end is too strong.

And besides, Liz thinks, what's the rush?

In the water, the swaddling fabric is stiff like plaster. Liz rocks back and forth trying to rip it. The motion does not free her, but it does turn her 180 degrees until she is facing into the current. All around her, babies float by.

The waves smack her exposed face. Salt stings her eyes. Water gets into her lungs. Liz feels her legs beginning to sink.

She leans her neck forward and tries to tear at the swaddling clothes with her teeth. After much effort, she succeeds in rip-ping the tiniest of holes, which allows her to rotate her shoulder over and over again. It hurts like hell, but she finally frees her left biceps, then her left forearm, then her hand. She reaches her hand above the surface of the water.

She struggles to pull herself out of the water with her free hand, but it's too late. Too much water has filled her lungs.

She sinks. It's a long way to the ocean floor. It gets darker and darker. Liz hits the bottom with a thud. A cloud of sand and other debris forms around her. And then she passes out.

When Liz wakes the next morning, she cannot move and she wonders if she is dead. But then she realizes she can open her eyes and her heart is beating, albeit very slowly. It occurs to Liz that she might be trapped at the bottom of the ocean forever. Neither dead nor alive. A ghost.

'Look, man, I'm sorry, but it's too late,' Curtis says to Owen. 'She's gone.'

'I just don't believe Liz would do something like this,' Owen replies, shaking his head. 'It just doesn't seem like her at all.'

Betty shakes her head, too. 'I can't believe it either.' She sighs. 'She was very depressed for a while when she first got here. I thought she was over it, but I guess she wasn't after all.'

'I'm going after her in my boat,' Owen says.

'She's gone. The launch nurse confirmed it. There's nothing we can do now.' Betty shoots Curtis a dirty look, and he looks away.

'I'm going after her in my boat,' Owen repeats.

'But—' Betty says.

'She might have changed her mind. And if she did, she might need our help,' Owen says.

'I'll come with you,' Curtis and Betty say at the same time.

For two days and two nights, they search all along the coasts of Elsewhere in Owen's little boat for any trace of Liz. She is nowhere to be found. On the second night, Owen tells Curtis and Betty to go home. 'I can do this myself,' he says.

'There's no point, Owen. I hate to say it, but she's gone. She's really, really gone. You should go home, too,' Betty says.

Owen shakes his head. 'No, I'm just going to give it one more day.'

With heavy hearts, Betty and Curtis agree to return home.

'Do you think we should have stayed with him?' Curtis asks Betty in her kitchen back at the house.

Betty sighs. 'I think he's trying to make peace. I think he *wanted* to be by himself.'

Curtis nods. 'I'm sorry I didn't come to you on Saturday night. We quarreled about it, and she swore me to secrecy.'

'It's not your fault. I should have known something was wrong. I only wish she had come to me.'

At that moment, Curtis spies a note tacked to the fridge with Betty's name on it. 'Look Betty, I think she may have left a note.'

Betty runs across the room and tears the note off the fridge. 'Why in the world didn't I see it before?'

Curtis looks out the window to give Betty some privacy while she reads. Less than a minute later, she slumps into a chair. 'It doesn't say why! It doesn't say anything actually,' she says tearfully. 'You spoke to her last. Why do you think she did it?'

'I'm not entirely sure,' he says after a moment. 'I think she felt she couldn't have a normal life here. She wanted to be an adult. She wanted to fall in love.'

'She could have fallen in love here!' Betty protests. 'I thought she already had.'

'I think that was part of the problem,' Curtis says delicately.

'But she could have fallen in love again! It could have been Owen or it could have been with someone entirely new.'

'I think she felt the conditions here were not likely to result in a lasting love,' Curtis explains.

Betty embraces Curtis. He gently sniffs her hair, which he thinks smells like a combination of roses and saltwater.

'Then again,' Curtis says softly, 'the conditions are rarely very good anywhere, but love still happens all the time.'

Liz realizes she will never be able to heal enough to swim back to the top. She will age backward just enough to keep alive and breathing, but unless someone finds her, she is for all practical purposes dead. Really dead, this time.

And yet she isn't dead either. Being dead would almost be preferable. She remembers a story Owen once told her of a man who had drowned on the way to the Well. No one found him for thirty years and when they finally located him, he was a baby, ready to go back to Earth.

If no one knows you're alive, no one you love, you may as well be dead, Liz thinks.

Liz stares above her, for there is nothing else to do at the bottom of the ocean.

On the second night Liz is underwater, two mermaids, a redhead and a blonde, swim by. They stop to look at Liz.

'Are you a mermaid?' the redhead asks Liz.

Liz cannot speak, because her larynx reflexively closed when she began to drown. She blinks her eyes twice.

'I don't think she is,' the blond mermaid says. 'See, it's a stupid thing who cannot even talk.'

'And she has very small breasts,' the redhead adds, laughing.

'I think it's a slug,' the blonde says.

'Oh, don't say that,' the redhead replies. 'I think you've hurt its feelings. Look, it's crying.'

'I don't care if it is. It's terribly dull. Let's go,' the blonde says. And the two mermaids swim happily away.

Mermaids (nasty, vain beasts) are one of the many creatures that live at the bottom of the ocean, in the land between Elsewhere and Earth.

At the Bottom of the Ocean, in the Land Between Elsewhere and Earth

On her third day underwater, Liz is woken by a strange sound. The sound could be a distant foghorn, or a low-pitched bell, or maybe even an engine. She opens her eyes. A familiar glint of silver flashes in the distance. Liz squints a little. It's a gondola! And then she sees that the gondola is etched onto a silver moon, and the moon is connected to a silver chain. And the sound is very like ticking. Liz's heart beats wildly. It's my old pocket watch, she thinks. Someone's fixed it, and if I can only reach up my arm, I can get it back.

And so she summons all her strength.

And so she lifts her one free hand.

But the watch is farther away than she first thought.

And so she summons a little more strength.

And so she peels away the swaddling clothes until her other hand is free.

And so she beats her arms.

But she can't swim without her feet.

And so she peels away more of the cloth until she is naked as the day she was born.

And so she is naked.

But, at last, her arms and her legs are free.

And so she begins to swim.

Liz swims and swims and swims and swims, always keeping the silver moon in sight. And the gondola grows larger and larger. And the rest of the watch seems to disappear. And Liz finally reaches the surface, gasping for air, gasping for life.

And when her eyes finally adjust to the daylight, the gondola is nowhere to be found. Instead, she sees a familiar white tugboat.

'Liz!' Owen yells. 'Are you all right?'

Liz can't speak. Her lungs are too filled with water, and she is freezing. Owen notices that her lips are blue.

He pulls her onto the boat and covers her with a blanket.

Liz coughs for the longest time, trying to expel the water from her lungs.

'Are you okay?' Owen asks.

'I seem to have lost my clothes,' Liz croaks, her voice scratchy and sore.

'I noticed.'

'And I almost died,' Liz says. 'Again,' she adds.

'I'm sorry.'

'And I'm totally pissed off at you,' Liz says.

'I'm sorry for that, too. I hope you'll forgive me someday.'

'We'll see,' she says.

'Shall I take you home now?'

Liz nods.

Exhausted, she lies down on the deck. The sun feels warm on her face. She thinks it is pleasant to be on a boat that is bound for home. She begins to feel better immediately.

'I might like to learn how to drive a boat,' Liz says when they are almost back.

'I could teach you, if you want,' Owen says. 'It's a lot like driving a car.'

'Who taught you to drive boats?' Liz asks.

'My grandfather. He was a ship captain here and back on Earth. He just retired.'

'You never mentioned you had a grandfather.'

'Well, he's about six years old now—'

'Wait, he wasn't the captain of the SS *Nile*, was he?'

'Yes. The Captain. Exactly,' Owen answers.

'That's the boat I was on! I met him the first day I got here!' Liz says.

'Small world,' Owen replies.

Restoration

Liz recuperates for two weeks at a healing center. Although she feels better after a few days, she enjoys her period of convalescence. It is nice to be tended to by one's friends and loved ones (especially when one's recovery is assured).

One of her visitors is Aldous Ghent. 'Well, my dear, it seems you are not on Earth,' he declares.

Liz nods. 'It seems that way.'

'This situation creates much paperwork, you know.' Aldous sighs and then smiles.

'I'm sorry.' Liz returns his smile.

'I'm not.' Aldous embraces Liz. He sniffles loudly.

'Aldous, you're crying!'

'My allergies again. I find they particularly act up during happy reunions.' Aldous blows his nose.

'I finally read *A Midsummer Night's Dream*,' Liz says.

'I thought one could only read Shakespeare for school.'

'I've had some free time lately.'

Aldous smiles. 'And your opinion?'

'It reminded me of here,' Liz replies.

'In what way?' Aldous prompts.

'You sound like a schoolteacher,' Liz admonishes him.

'Well, thank you very much. I used to be one, you know. You were saying, Elizabeth?'

Liz thinks for a moment. 'Well, there's this fairy world, and then there's the real world. And the way Shakespeare writes it, there's really no difference between the two. The fairies are just like real people with human problems and everything. And the human people and the fairies live side by side. They're together and they're apart. And the fairy world might be a dream, but the real world could be a dream also. I liked that.' Liz shrugs. 'I've never been much good at this English stuff. My best subjects used to be biology and algebra.'

'Fine subjects, indeed.'

'I'm reading *Hamlet* now,' Liz says. 'But I can already tell I don't like it as much as *Midsummer*.'

'No?'

'Well, Hamlet's so obsessed with dying, like that's gonna solve anything.' Liz shakes her head. 'If he only knew what we know.'

'If he only knew!' Aldous agrees.

One day, Curtis Jest visits.

'Lizzie,' Curtis says in a more serious voice than Liz has ever heard him use, 'I must ask you a question.'

'Yes, what is it?'

'It's about Betty,' Curtis whispers.

'What about her?' Liz asks.

'Has she any gentleman callers?' Curtis's whisper grows even softer.

'No, I don't think so, and why are we whispering?' Liz asks.

'Is there a *Grandpa* Betty in the picture?' Curtis continues to whisper.

'No, Grandpa Jake is remarried and lives on a boat near Monterey, California.'

Curtis takes a deep breath. 'So you're saying I might have a chance?'

'Curtis, a chance at what?'

'A chance with Betty.'

'A chance with Betty?' Liz repeats loudly.

'Liz, lower your voice. For God's sake, I am telling you this in confidence.' Curtis's eyes dart around the room. 'I find your grandmother a most delightful creature.'

'Curtis, are you saying you *like* Betty?' Liz whispers.

'I am a bit smitten with her. Yes, yes, you could say that.'

'Isn't Betty a bit old for you?' Liz asks. 'She was fifty when she died, you know. And she's around thirty-three now.'

'Yes, exactly! She has so much wisdom! And warmth! And, for now at least, I *am* twenty-nine years old myself. Do you think she will find me too immature?'

'No, Betty's not like that.' Liz smiles. 'Tell me one thing. Does she know yet?'

'No, not yet, but I was thinking I might write her a song.'

'Curtis, I think that's a wonderful idea.' Liz smiles again. 'Oh, and if you run out of things to say, compliment her garden.'

'Yes, yes, her garden! I shall, and I thank you very much for the tip, Lizzie.'

When Liz is allowed to return to Betty's house, she passes the days lazily in Betty's garden and continues to recover. Liz reclines on the hammock while Betty tends to her garden.

Without meaning to, Betty makes frequent stops just to check that Liz is still in the hammock where she should be.

'I'm not going anywhere,' Liz assures her.

Betty inhales sharply. 'It's just I thought I had lost you forever.'

'Oh, Betty, don't you know there's no such thing as forever?' Liz swings in her hammock, and Betty returns to her gardening. Five minutes later, they are interrupted all over again by Curtis Jest.

Curtis is strangely attired in a white suit and dark round sunglasses.

'Hello, Lizzie,' he says stiffly. 'Hello, Betty,' he says softly.

'Hello, Curtis,' Liz mimics his tone.

Curtis winks at Liz. Liz rolls over in the hammock and pretends to go to sleep. Sadie curls up behind Liz. Since Liz's return, Sadie has stayed as close to Liz as possible.

'My, Betty,' Curtis says, removing his sunglasses, 'you do have a lovely garden!'

'Thank you, Mr. Jest,' Betty replies.

'Would you mind if I stayed a while?' Curtis asks.

'Liz is asleep, and I was just going inside.'

'Oh, do you have to?'

'I do.'

'Maybe some other day, then,' Curtis stammers. 'Good day, Betty. My regards to Lizzie.'

Betty nods. 'Good day.'

'Oh, Betty,' Liz says as soon as Curtis is out of earshot, 'you were very cruel to Curtis.'

'You were the one who fell asleep as soon as he arrived.'

'I think he came to see you,' Liz admits.

'Me? Why on earth?'

'I think he had, um'–Liz pauses–'come to court.'

'Court!' Betty laughs. 'Why, that is the most perfectly absurd thing I've ever heard! Curtis Jest is a boy, and I'm old enough to be his–'

'Girlfriend,' Liz finishes. 'You're only about four biological years apart actually.'

'Darling, I'm through with romance, and I have been for some time.'

'Saying you're through with romance is like saying you're done with living, Betty. Life is better with a little romance, you know.'

'After everything, you can still say that?' Betty raises an eyebrow.

Liz smiles a little and chooses to ignore Betty's question. 'Give Curtis a chance, Betty.'

'I highly doubt I'll break his heart if I don't. I'm sure he'll have given up by tomorrow,' Betty says skeptically.

A week later, Betty and Liz are awakened in the middle of the night by the sounds of an acoustic guitar.

'This one's for you, Betty,' Curtis yells from the garden below.

He begins to sing for the first time in almost two years. It's a new song, one Liz has never heard before, one that will later come to be known as 'The Betty Song.'

By no means is it Curtis Jest's best performance, nor is it his finest moment as a songwriter. The lyrics are (it must be said) rather trite, mainly about the transformative powers of love. In truth, most love songs are exactly the same way.

Owen is devoted to Liz during her recuperation. He visits her every day.

'Liz,' Owen asks, 'when you were at the bottom of the ocean, what gave you the strength to come back up?'

'I thought I saw my watch floating on the surface, but it turned out to be your boat.'

'What watch?' Owen asks after a moment.

'When I lived on Earth, I had this watch. It needed to be fixed actually.'

Owen shakes his head. 'A broken watch brought you back?'

Liz shrugs. 'I know it might not seem so important.'

'You can get a new watch on Elsewhere you know.'

'Maybe.' Liz shrugs again.

The next day, Owen gives Liz a gold watch. Her old one was silver, but Liz doesn't tell him that. The new one is also not a pocket watch. It is a ladies' watch with a band made of tiny golden links. It is not the sort of thing Liz would normally choose for herself, but she doesn't tell him that either.

'Thank you,' Liz replies as Owen clasps the bracelet around her narrow wrist.

'It matches your hair,' Owen says, proud of the little gold

watch.

'Thank you very much,' Liz repeats.

That same afternoon, Jen visits Liz. (She had returned to Owen's after Emily left for keeper-of-books training.)

'Did you like the watch?' Jen asks. 'I helped Owen pick it out.'

'It's really nice,' Liz says, scratching Jen between the ears.

'He wasn't sure whether to get silver or gold, but I told him gold. Gold's a great color, don't you think?' asks Jen.

'The best,' Liz agrees. 'Say, Jen, aren't dogs supposed to be color-blind?'

'No. Who ever said that?'

'It's something they say about dogs on Earth.'

'Those Earth people are funny that way,' Jen says, shaking her head. 'How do they know if we're color-blind if they never even ask us? I mean, they can't even speak the language.'

'Good point,' Liz says.

'Back on Earth, I once saw this television report that said dogs had no emotions. Can you believe that?' Jen cocks her head. 'Say, Liz, I wanted to thank you for letting me stay with you all that time.'

'It was no trouble.'

'And I'm sorry for that time'—Jen lowers her voice—'I peed in your bed.'

'It's forgotten,' Liz reassures Jen.

'Oh good! I couldn't bear it if you were mad at me.'

Liz shakes her head. 'I wasn't mad at you.'

'Owen's much better now,' the dog says. 'He's learning to speak Canine and everything.'

'You aren't mad at him, even a little?' Liz asks.

'Maybe a tiny bit at first, but not anymore. I know he's a good person. And he said he was sorry. And I love him. And when you love a person, you have to forgive him sometimes. And that's what I think.'

Liz nods. 'That's a good philosophy,' Liz says.

'Would you mind rubbing my belly?' Jen asks, flipping happily onto her back.

Later that night, Liz stares at the gold watch. Ah well, Liz thinks to herself. The watch isn't exactly like the old one, or anything like it, for that matter. But the intention is good. Liz shakes her wrist, causing the links to make a pleasing bell-like tinkle. She puts her wrist to her ear and enjoys the tick of the second hand. Five ticks later, Liz resolves to forgive the watch for its imperfections. She kisses its face with tenderness. Really, what a marvelous gift, she thinks.

Before long, Liz forgives Owen, too. Yes, he is flawed, but he is also an excellent driving teacher. If you are going to forgive a person, Liz decides, it is best to do it sooner rather than later. Later, Liz knows from experience, could be sooner than you thought.

Part III: Antique Lands

Time Passes

There will be other lives.

There will be other lives for nervous boys with sweaty palms, for bittersweet fumblings in the backseats of cars, for caps and gowns in royal blue and crimson, for mothers clasping pretty pearl necklaces around daughters' unlined necks, for your full name read aloud in an auditorium, for brand-new suitcases transporting you to strange new people in strange new lands.

And there will be other lives for unpaid debts, for one-night stands, for Prague and for Paris, for painful shoes with pointy toes, for indecisions and revisions.

And there will be other lives for fathers walking daughters down aisles.

And there will be other lives for sweet babies with skin like milk.

And there will be other lives for a man you don't recognize, for a face in a mirror that is no longer yours, for the funerals of intimates, for shrinking, for teeth that fall out, for hair on your chin, for forgetting everything. Everything.

Oh, there are so many lives. How we wish we could live them concurrently instead of one by one by one. We could select the best pieces of each, stringing them together like a strand of pearls. But that's not how it works. A human's life is a beautiful mess.

In the year Liz will turn thirteen again, she whispers in Betty's ear, 'Happiness is a choice.'

'So, what's your choice?' Betty asks.

Liz closes her eyes, and in a split second she chooses.

Five years pass.

When one is happy, time passes quickly. Liz feels as if one evening she went to bed fourteen and the next morning she woke up nine.

Two Weddings

Someone from Earth's been trying to Contact you,' Owen announces one evening after work. Now the head of the Bureau of Supernatural Crime and Contact, he is usually one of the first people on Elsewhere to know about these matters.

'What?' Liz barely looks up from her book. Recently, she has taken to rereading her favorite books from when she first learned to read on Earth.

'What are you reading?' Owen asks.

'*Charlotte's Web*,' Liz says. 'It's really sad. One of the main characters just died.'

'You ought to read the book from end to beginning,' Owen jokes. 'That way, no one dies, and it's always a happy ending.'

'That's about the dumbest thing I've ever heard.' Liz rolls her eyes and returns to her reading.

'Aren't you at all interested in who's trying to Contact you?'

Owen asks. From his coat pocket, he removes a green recorked wine bottle with a sticky palimpsest where the label had once been. Inside the bottle is a rolled-up ecru envelope. (The envelope is really more pleated than rolled, because of the thickness of the paper.) 'It washed up on the wharf today,' Owen says, handing the bottle to Liz. 'The boys over in Earth Artifacts had to uncork it to see who it was for, but the contents of the envelope haven't been touched. When we get an MIB, we try as much as possible to preserve the person's privacy.'

'What's an MIB?' Liz asks, setting her book aside to examine the bottle.

'Message in a bottle,' Owen answers. 'It's one of the few ways to get mail from Earth to Elsewhere. No one knows exactly why it works, but it does.'

'I've never gotten one before,' Liz says.

'They're not as common as they used to be.'

'Why's that?' Liz asks.

'People on Earth don't write letters so much anymore. Messages in bottles probably don't occur to them. And it's not always a sure thing.'

Liz uncorks the bottle. She removes the thick envelope, which is remarkably well preserved considering its watery voyage. On the front is an address in elegant calligraphy done with a rich, black-green ink:

Miss Elizabeth 'Liz' 'Lizzie' Marie Hall and Guest Heaven

or

The Undiscovered Country or
The Shadowlands or

The Big Sleep or
The Great Unknown or
The Great Beyond or
Elysian Fields or
Valhalla or
Fortunate Isles or
Isle of the Blessed or
The Kingdom of Joy and Light or
Paradise or
Eden or
The Firmament or
The Sky or
Wherever you are, whatever it's called

'Very thorough,' Owen says, 'but they never write Elsewhere.'

'No one on Earth calls it that,' Liz reminds him. She turns the envelope over. The return address is in the same calligraphy:

192 Reed Street
Medford, Ma 02109

'That's Zooey's address,' Liz says as she lifts the flap. Inside, she finds a three-paneled ecru wedding invitation and a long handwritten note. Liz slips the note into her pocket.

' "You are invited to the wedding of Zooey Anne Brandon and Paul Scott Spencer," ' Liz reads aloud. 'My best friend's getting married?'

'You mean your best friend before you met me, right?' Owen teases her.

Liz ignores him. 'The wedding's the first weekend in June. That's in less than two weeks.' Liz tosses the invitation aside. 'She certainly took her time inviting me,' Liz huffs.

'You should probably forgive her. It's pretty hard to send things here, you know? She probably sent this months ago.' Owen picks up the invitation. 'Good-quality paper stock.'

'Isn't she too young to get married?' Liz asks. 'She's my age.' Liz corrects herself, 'I mean, she was my age. Actually, she was a month older than me, so I guess that makes her almost twenty-two.'

Owen takes out a pen and begins filling out the response card. 'Will madam be bringing a guest?'

'No,' Liz replies.

'What about me?' asks Owen, his eyes wide with mock offense.

'Sorry to disappoint, O,' Liz says, taking the response card from him, 'but I think we'd have a little trouble making travel arrangements.' She carefully slips the response card and the invitation back into the envelope.

'We could watch from the OD,' Owen suggests.

'I don't want to watch,' Liz says.

'Then we could dive,' Owen says. 'From the Well, you could congratulate her and everything.'

'I can't believe you're even suggesting that.' Liz shakes her head. 'In your line of work.'

'Oh come on, Liz! Where's your sense of adventure? One last hurrah before we're too young for any more hurrahs! What do you say?'

Liz thinks for a moment before she answers. 'When I died,

Zooey didn't go to my funeral, so I see no need to attend her wedding.'

That night in bed, Liz reads Zooey's note. She notices that Zooey's handwriting is the same as when they were both fifteen and used to pass notes in school.

Dear Liz,

It's pretty crazy for me to write you after all this time, but as you can see, I'm getting married! :) I've missed you a lot. I wonder where you are, and what you've been doing. And in case you've wondered about me, I'm in my first year of law school, here in Chicago where I live now.

So if you have the time and the inclination, and if you happen to be in Boston (we wanted Chicago, but Mom won), you should drop by the wedding. The boy's name is Paul, and he smells good, and he has nice forearms.

I know you probably won't ever get this letter (sort of feels like writing to Santa which is really bizarre considering I'm Jewish), but it was worth a shot. I already tried a psychic medium and Rabbi Singer of Congregation B'nai B'rith, where my parents still attend services back in Brookline. Incidentally, Mom and Dad say "hi." It was Paul's idea to put the invite in the bottle. I think he got it from a movie, though.

Love,

Your Best Friend on Earth (I hope),

Zooey

P.S. I'm sorry I didn't go to your funeral.

'I want to give a toast,' Liz announces to Owen the next

morning.

'By all means,' Owen says, sitting down with his cup of coffee. 'I'm all ears.'

'Not now, silly,' Liz replies. 'I meant at Zooey's wedding. Your idea to go to the Well might not be as bad as I first thought.'

'So you're saying you want to dive?' Owen's eyes light up.

'Yes, and I need you to help me with the toast. The last time I tried to communicate from the Well was a bit of a disaster,' Liz says.

'That was the night you met me, I believe.'

'Like I said, it was a bit of a disaster,' Liz jokes.

'That isn't funny.' Owen shakes his head.

Liz continues, 'All the faucets in the house turned on, and—'

'Beginner's mistake,' Owen interrupts.

'And nobody could understand what I was saying,' Liz finishes.

'And you were arrested,' Owen adds.

'That, too,' Liz concedes. 'So how do I make it so the people at the wedding will understand me and not run from the room screaming?'

'Well, for one, you have to remember not to scream. Once you have their attention, whispering is much more effective. Screaming ghosts scare people, you know,' Owen says.

'Good tip.'

'And you have to pick a running water source and focus on it. And good breath control is a must,' Owen says. 'I'll come with you, of course, but only if you want me to.'

'Won't you get sacked if they know you're helping me make Contact?'

Owen shrugs. 'I'm head of the whole department now, and people tend to look the other way.'

Liz smiles. 'Then I guess it's settled.' She raises her glass of orange juice. 'To our dive!' she proclaims.

'To our dive!' Owen repeats, raising his cup of coffee. 'I love an adventure, don't you?'

The evening of Zooey's wedding reception, Owen and Liz meet at the beach at eight o'clock. The reception starts at eight-thirty, and the dive itself should take forty minutes by Owen's calculations.

'Once we get there, you only have a little over half an hour,' Owen warns her. 'I've told the boys from work to pick us up at nine-thirty.'

'Do you think that's long enough?' Liz worries.

'It isn't good to spend too much time down there. It *is* still illegal, you know.'

Liz nods.

'I don't mean to be rude, but your wet suit's a bit loose in the bottom, Liz,' Owen says.

'Is it?' She tugs at the stretchy fabric around her butt. 'The wet suit's getting old. I haven't used it in almost six years.'

'You look like you're wearing a diaper.'

'Yeah, well, I guess I'm shrinking, too. I am nine, you know,' Liz says.

'That's little.'

'Well, I'm actually nine–six, and I would have been twenty-one, so that's not the same as being plain nine,' Liz says. 'Besides, Owen, you're eleven. That's not much older than nine.'

'I'm eleven?' Owen asks. 'I certainly don't feel eleven.'

'Well, you certainly act eleven a lot of the time,' Liz teases.

'And if I'd lived, I would have been forty-one,' Owen adds.

'Wow, that's really old!' Liz shakes her head. 'Imagine! If you were forty-one, and I was twenty-one, and we still lived on Earth, we probably never would have met.'

The dive passes without incident. Having made it many times before, Owen is an excellent guide.

When they get to the Well, they can find only one running water source with a view into the reception—a large outdoor fountain across a courtyard. From this location, they can mostly see through the tall glass windows that line the walls of the ballroom where Zooey's reception is being held.

'We aren't very close,' Liz complains. 'If I had only wanted to watch, we could have just gone to the OD.'

'Don't worry. We'll find a better place for you to make your toast from,' Owen assures her.

Across the courtyard and through the windows, Liz sees a wedding party much like every other one she has ever seen: abundant yellow roses, bridesmaids' dresses in pink, a bored-looking wedding singer, Zooey in an off-white A-line dress, the groom in a gray tuxedo with tails. Liz sees Zooey's mother and father among the crowd. And behind them, she sees her own mother and father.

'Look, Owen, it's my mom and dad. Dad looks older, and Mom changed her hair,' Liz says. 'Hi, Mom! Hi, Dad!' Liz waves.

242

'Oh, and there's my brother! Hi, Alvy!'

'Which one's Zooey?' Owen asks.

'Duh,' Liz replies, 'she's the one in the white dress.'

'Oh, right!'

Liz rolls her eyes. 'You're definitely getting stupider as you get younger, O.' Liz looks at Zooey. Zooey is twenty-one, a woman. How odd, Liz thinks, that I'm nine and she's twenty-one.

'We really should start looking for a place for you to toast from,' Owen says. 'We've only got about twenty-five minutes left.'

First, they try the bathroom sink.

'CONGRATULATIONS, ZOOEY! THIS IS ELIZABETH MARIE HALL!' Liz yells. But the bathroom is too far away, and no one hears her.

'Maybe I'll wait until she comes in here?' Liz says to Owen. 'At least then I'd get to talk to her.'

'Not enough time. And brides always complain that they never get to eat or go to the bathroom. Let's try the kitchen,' Owen suggests.

The kitchen, while slightly closer to the reception area, is incredibly noisy with staff and plates and timers and other kitchen sounds.

'I LOVE YOU, ZOOEY! CONGRATULATIONS TO YOU AND PAUL,' Liz yells again, this time from the kitchen sink.

A busboy screams and drops a tray filled with dirty salad plates.

'SORRY,' Liz apologizes. 'This is getting ridiculous,' Liz says to Owen. 'All I've succeeded in doing is scaring a waiter. We have to find somewhere closer.'

In a burst of desperation, Liz suggests the samovar, but Owen, who knows more about these things, rejects the idea on the grounds that the water source has to be connected to actual plumbing. Despite Owen's warnings against it, Liz tries the coffee pot, but it doesn't work anyway. (She's glad it doesn't work—she would have felt entirely stupid giving a toast from a coffee pot.)

'Oh, let's just go back to the fountain,' Liz says dejectedly. 'Maybe if we both yell together, she'll hear us.'

'CONGRATULATIONS! CONGRATULATIONS! CONGRATULATIONS!' Owen and Liz scream from the fountain.

They continue yelling for five more minutes, but no one hears them over the noise from the fountain and through the walls. 'Well,' Liz says with a sigh, 'at least I got to see Zooey in her wedding dress. We could have just done that from the ODs, I suppose.'

'But it wouldn't have been as much fun,' Owen points out.

'Should we swim back?' Liz asks.

'No, we might as well just wait,' Owen says. 'The boat'll be here in about ten minutes anyway.'

While they wait, Liz watches Zooey's reception inside the ballroom. From their position at the fountain, she can see her own mother and father dancing.

'Your mom looks like you,' Owen observes.

'Mom's hair is darker. She actually looks more like Alvy than . . .' Liz's voice trails off. Out of the corner of her eye, she sees Alvy leave the reception hall through the side door. He's walking toward the fountain.

244

'Liz?' Owen asks.

'I think my brother's coming this way,' Liz says.

Alvy walks right up to the fountain and looks into the water. Liz holds her breath.

'Lizzie,' Alvy whispers to the fountain.

'Remember,' Owen says, 'don't yell.'

'It's me,' Liz whispers.

'I thought I heard you,' Alvy says. 'First I thought it was coming from the bathroom. And then the kitchen. And then out here.'

Liz's eyes well up a little bit. Good old Alvy. 'Alvy, it's so good to talk to you.'

'I'll go get Zooey! You're here to congratulate her, right? I'll go get Mom and Dad, too,' Alvy says. 'They'll definitely want to talk to you.'

Owen shakes his head. 'The guys are going to be here in five minutes.'

'There isn't time, Alvy,' Liz says. 'Just give Zooey and Mom and Dad my love. In a way that won't freak them out, of course.'

'I'll just run in real quick and get them.'

'No!' Liz says. 'I might not be here when you get back. Let's just talk a little bit, you and me. I have to go soon.'

'Okay,' Alvy agrees.

'How's eighth grade?' she asks.

'I'm in ninth actually. I skipped.'

'Alvy, that's awesome! You were always so smart. How's ninth grade, then?'

'It's cool,' Alvy says. 'I'm in debate this year, which is definitely better than band, which I was in last year. God, Lizzie, you don't actually want to know about this stuff, do you?'

'I do. I totally do.'

Alvy shakes his head. 'I think about you, you know?'

'I think about you, too.'

'Is it okay where you are?'

'It's different.'

'Different how?'

'It's'—she pauses—'hard to explain. It's not like you think. But it's okay here. I'm okay, Alvy.'

'Are you happy?' Alvy asks.

And for the second time since she came to Elsewhere, Liz pauses and considers this question. 'I am,' she says. 'I have a lot of friends. And I have a dog called Sadie. And I see Betty. She's our grandma, the one who died. You'd like her so much. Her sense of humor is like yours. I miss you guys all the time. Oh God, Alvy, there's so much I want to talk to you about!'

'I know! There's so much I want to tell you and ask you, too, but I can't remember what.'

'I'm sorry about that time with the sweater.'

'You aren't still thinking about that, are you?' Alvy shrugs. 'Don't even mention it. It all worked out.'

'I'm sorry if I got you in trouble.'

'Please. Mom and Dad were total disasters after you died. Everything set them off. I know the sweater definitely helped Dad.'

'I'm sorry if it's been hard for you, then. Hard because of me.'

'Lizzie, the only thing that's been hard is missing my sister.'

'You have such a good heart. Do you know that? You were always the best kid in the world. If I was ever annoyed at you or anything, it's just 'cause you were so much younger than me and also I was used to being an only child.'

'I know that, Lizzie, and I love you, too.'

Owen hears the sound of the net coming toward them. Owen whispers to Liz, 'They're almost here.'

'Who's with you?' Alvy asks.

'That's Owen. He's my'—she pauses—'boyfriend.'

Alvy nods. 'Cool.'

'Nice to meet you, Alvy,' Owen says.

'We met before, didn't we? Your voice is familiar. You were the guy who told me the right closet.' Alvy asks.

'Yup,' Owen says, 'that was me.'

'By the way, Alvy,' Liz asks, 'how did you ever hear me tonight?'

'I always listen to the water. I've been listening since I was little,' Alvy says. 'I could never stop hoping it might be you.'

At that moment, Liz feels a familiar net pulling her and Owen away from the Well.

Liz sighs. So the wedding wasn't exactly like she imagined it would be. But then, what in life is?

'Your brother is a really cool kid,' Owen says on the ride back up.

'He is,' Liz agrees. 'All things considered, it was a nice wedding, don't you think?'

'It was,' Owen agrees.

'And Zooey was beautiful,' Liz adds.

Owen shrugs. 'I didn't really get a good chance to look at her. All brides look about the same anyway.'

Liz latches her fingers into the net. 'Sometimes I wish I could get a white dress.'

'You have a white dress, Liz,' says Owen, 'though it's more like pajamas.'

'You know what I mean. A wedding dress.'

The net is approaching the surface. Just as they are about to hit the cool night air, Owen turns to Liz. 'I'll marry you, if you want,' he says.

'I'm too young now,' she replies.

'I would have married you before, but you didn't want to,' he says.

'I was too young before, and we didn't know each other well enough.'

'Oh,' says Owen.

'Besides,' says Liz, 'there didn't seem to be much of a point. You had been married before, and we already knew what we were, I guess.'

'Oh,' says Owen, 'but I would have, you know.'

'I know you would have,' says Liz, 'and knowing you would have was nearly as good.' At that moment, the net surfaces and they are lowered onto the deck of a tugboat.

'Hey, boss,' a detective for the bureau asks Owen, 'you want to drive back?'

Owen looks at Liz. 'It's fine if you want to drive,' Liz says. 'I'm sleepy anyway.' Liz yawns. It had been a great day, she thinks. She walks over to a pile of raincoats and lies down.

Owen watches as Liz uses one of the raincoats as a blanket. Right then, he decides to tell Liz that he wants to marry her to-morrow or next weekend or sometime really soon. 'Liz,' he calls out. But the boat is too loud, and Liz can't hear him, and the subject never comes up again.

The following Monday, Curtis Jest visits Liz at the Division of Domestic Animals. It's rather unusual for Curtis to come to her work, but Liz doesn't say anything.

'How was the wedding?' Curtis asks Liz.

'About average,' Liz replies, 'but I enjoyed it very much. It's good to see people you haven't seen for a while.'

Curtis nods.

'But all weddings are about the same, aren't they? Flowers and tuxedoes and white dresses and cake and coffee.' Liz laughs. 'In a way, it hardly seems worth it.'

Curtis nods again. Liz looks at him. She notices that he is unusually pale.

'Curtis, what is it?'

Curtis takes a deep breath. Liz has never seen him this nervous. 'That's just it, Lizzie. It does barely seem worth it, unless it happens to be your wedding.'

'I don't understand.'

'I've come'–Curtis clears his throat–'I've come to ask your permission–'

'My permission? For what?'

'Stop interrupting, Liz! This is hard enough,' Curtis says. 'I've come to ask your permission to marry Betty.'

'You want to marry Betty? My Betty?' Liz stammers.

'I've been seeing her for five years, as you know, and I was recently overcome by the utter conviction that I had to be her husband,' Curtis says. 'You're her closest relative, so I felt I should run it by you first.'

Liz throws her arms around Curtis. 'Good Lord, Curtis. Congratulations!'

'She hasn't said yes, yet,' Curtis replies.

'Do you think she will?' Liz asks.

'We can only hope, my dear. We can only hope.' Curtis crosses his fingers. He keeps them crossed until Betty says yes almost two days later.

The wedding is planned for the last week in August, two weeks after what would have been Liz's twenty-second birthday.

Betty asks Liz to be her maid of honor. Thandi is the other bridesmaid, and the two girls wear matching dresses in deep golden silk shantung that Betty sewed herself.

The wedding takes place in Betty's garden. At Betty's request, no flowers are harmed for the union.

Betty cries, and Curtis cries, and Owen cries, and Thandi cries, and Sadie cries, and Jen cries, and Aldous Ghent cries. But Liz doesn't cry. She's too happy to cry. Two of her favorite people in the world are getting married, and that doesn't happen every day.

After the ceremony is over, Curtis sings the song he wrote for Betty when Liz was recuperating.

Liz walks over to Thandi, who is eating an enormous piece of wedding cake.

'The first time I saw you I thought you looked like a queen,' Liz says to Thandi.

'Didn't stop you from waking me up, though,' Thandi replies.

'You remember that?' Liz asks. 'You were barely awake at the time.'

'Not much I forget, Liz. My memory's long long long.' Thandi smiles, revealing two missing front teeth.

'What happened to your teeth?' Liz asks.

Thandi shrugs. 'Fell out. We're not getting any older, you know.'

'Isn't nine a little old to be losing your adult teeth?'

'Mine came in late the first time,' Thandi replies.

Liz nods. 'Getting younger is odd, isn't it?'

'Not really. Just feels like all the unimportant stuff is falling away. Like a snake shedding its skin, really.' Thandi takes another bite of cake. 'Being old is so heavy, really. I feel lighter every day. Sometimes, I feel like I could fly away.'

'Does it ever feel like a dream to you?' Liz asks.

'Oh no!' Thandi shakes her head. 'We're not starting that again, are we?'

Liz laughs. Curtis Jest begins singing an old Machine song. 'I love this song,' Liz says. 'I'm going to ask Owen to dance with me.'

'You do that, dream girl.' Thandi smiles and takes another bite of her cake.

Liz locates Owen quickly.

'I was looking for you,' he says.

'Let's dance,' she says, pulling Owen to the makeshift dance floor in the middle of Betty's garden.

Owen and Liz dance. From across the room, Betty holds up her champagne flute.

'Mazel tov,' Liz calls to her.

'You look pretty today,' Owen whispers in Liz's ear. 'I like your dress.'

Liz shrugs. 'It's just a dress.'

'Well, it's definitely better than your wet suit.'

Liz laughs. She closes her eyes. She listens to the music and smells the sweet fragrances of Betty's garden. A cool wind blows Liz's bridesmaid dress against her legs, sweeping summer away.

For better or worse, this is my life, she thinks.

This is my life.

My life.

The Change

In the year Liz turns eight, Sadie becomes a puppy again.

In the months leading up to her Release, Sadie grows smaller, her fur becomes softer, her breath sweeter, her eyes clearer. She speaks less and less until she doesn't speak at all. Before her teeth fall out, she chews up several of Liz's books. Although Sadie spends most of her time napping in Betty's garden, she has strange bursts of manic activity where all she wants to do is wrestle with Paco and Jen. Both older dogs tolerate Sadie's outbursts with considerable equanimity.

In the weeks before her Release, Sadie becomes so small you can barely tell she is a puppy. She might have been a large mouse. Her eyes seal closed, and Liz has to feed her tiny drops of milk from her pinky. Sadie still seems to recognize her name when Liz says it.

On the dawn of the Release, Liz and Owen drive Sadie to the River. It is the first Release Liz has attended since her own aborted attempt six years ago.

At sunrise, a wind begins to blow. The current carries the babies faster and faster down the River, back to Earth. Liz watches Sadie in the current for as long as possible. Sadie becomes a dot, then a speck, then nothing at all.

On the drive home, Owen notices that Liz is unusually quiet. 'You're sad about Sadie,' he says.

Liz shakes her head. She hasn't cried and she doesn't feel particularly sad. Not that she feels happy either. In truth, she hasn't felt much of anything aside from a general tightness in her belly, as if her stomach is making a fist. 'No,' Liz replies, 'not sad exactly.'

'What is it, then?' Owen asks.

'I'm not all that sad,' Liz says, 'because Sadie hadn't been Sadie for a while, and I knew this would happen eventually.' Liz pauses, trying to precisely articulate her feelings. 'What I am is a mix of scared, happy, and excited, I think.'

'All those things at once?' Owen asks.

'Yes. I'm happy and excited because it's nice to think of my friend somewhere on Earth. I like thinking of a dog, who won't be called Sadie, but will still be my Sadie all the same.'

'You said scared, too.'

'I worry about the people that will take care of her on Earth. I hope they'll be nice to her, and treat her with good humor and love, and brush her coat, and feed her things other than kibble, because she gets bored always eating the same thing.' Liz sighs. 'It's such a terribly dangerous thing being a baby when you think about it. So much can go wrong.'

Owen kisses Liz gently on the forehead, 'Sadie will be fine.'

'You don't know that!' Liz protests. 'Sadie could end up with people who keep her cooped up all day, or put cigarette butts in her coat.' Liz's eyes tear at the thought.

'I know that Sadie will be fine,' Owen says calmly.

'But how do you know?'

'I know,' he says, 'because I choose to believe it is so.'

Liz rolls her eyes. 'Sometimes, Owen, you can be so totally full of it.'

Owen's feelings are hurt. He doesn't speak to Liz for the rest of the car ride home.

Later that night, Liz weeps for Sadie. She weeps so loudly she wakes Betty.

'Oh, doll,' Betty says, 'you can get another dog if you want. I know it won't be Sadie, but . . .'

'No,' Liz replies through her tears. 'I can't. I just can't.'

'Are you sure?'

'I'll never have another dog,' Liz says firmly, 'and please don't ever, ever, ever mention it to me again.'

A month later, Liz changes her mind when an aged pug named Lucy arrives in Elsewhere. At thirteen years old, Lucy had finally died peacefully in her sleep, in Liz's childhood room. (Liz's possessions had been boxed up years ago, but Lucy never stopped sleeping there.)

From the shore, Liz watches Lucy, slightly arthritic and grayer in the face, waddle down the boardwalk. She waddles right up to Liz and wags her loosely curled tail three times. She cocks her head, squinting up at Liz with bulging brown eyes.

'Where've you been?' Lucy asks.

'I died,' Liz answers in Canine.

'Oh right, I tried not to think about that too much. I just pre-tended you went to college early and didn't visit very often.' Lucy nods her sweet wrinkly head. 'We missed you a lot, you know. Alvy, Olivia, Arthur, and me.'

'I missed you guys, too.' Liz lifts Lucy up from the ground and holds the heavy little lapdog in her arms.

'You've gained weight,' Liz teases.

'Only a pound or two or maybe three, no more than that,' Lucy answers. 'Personally, I think I look better with a little heft.'

'Multum in parvo,' Liz jokes. It's Latin, meaning "much in little." This is the pug motto and a favorite joke of Liz's family because of Lucy's tendency to gain weight.

'Liz,' Lucy asks, squinting up at the sky, 'is this *up there*? Is this . . . heaven?'

'I don't know,' Liz answers.

'It isn't "down there," is it?'

'I certainly don't think so.' Liz laughs.

The dog gently sniffs the air. 'Well, it smells a lot like Earth,' she concludes, 'only a bit saltier.'

'It's good that you can speak so well now,' Lucy whispers in Liz's ear. 'I have so much to tell you about everything and every-body.'

Liz smiles. 'I can't wait.'

'But first, let's get something to eat, and then take a nap. And a bath, then a nap. Then something else to eat, and maybe a walk. But then definitely something else to eat.'

Liz sets Lucy on the ground, and the two walk home with Lucy chattering away.

Amadou

On the same day Liz retires from the Division of Domestic Animals, a man she knows very well, but has never before met, stops by her office. The man looks different in person than he did through the binoculars. His eyes are softer, but the lines between his eyebrows are more pronounced.

'I am Amadou Bonamy.' He speaks precisely, with a slight French-Haitian accent.

Liz takes a deep breath before answering. 'I know who you are.'

Amadou notices the balloons from Liz's retirement party. 'You are having a celebration. I will come back,' he says.

'The party is for my retirement. If you come back, you won't find me again. Please come in.'

Amadou nods. 'I recently died of cancer,' he says. 'It was lung cancer. I did not smoke, but my father did.'

Liz nods.

'I have not driven a cab for many years. I finished college at night and I became a teacher.'

Liz nods again.

'All these years, I have felt despair as you cannot imagine. I hit you with my cab and I did not stop.'

'You called the hospital from a pay phone, right?' Liz asks.

Amadou nods. He looks down at his shoes.

'I've thought about it more than anybody, I guess. I've thought about it, and stopping probably wouldn't have made a difference anyway,' Liz says, placing her hand on Amadou's arm.

There are tears in Amadou's eyes. 'I kept wishing I would get caught.'

'It wasn't your fault,' Liz says. 'I didn't look both ways.'

'You must tell me honestly. Has your life been very bad here?'

Liz thinks about Amadou's question before she answers. 'No. My life has been good actually.'

'But you must have missed many things?'

'As I've come to see it, my life would have been either here or elsewhere anyway,' Liz replies.

'Is that a joke?' Amadou asks.

'If it amuses you, it is.' Liz laughs a little. 'So, Amadou, may I ask you why you didn't stop that day? I've always wanted to know.'

'This is no excuse, but my little boy had been very sick. The medical bills were astounding. If I had lost the cab or your parents had asked for money, I did not know what would have happened to me or my family. I was desperate. Of course, this is no excuse.' Amadou shakes his head. 'Can you ever forgive me?'

'I forgave you long ago,' Liz says.

'But you were so young,' Amadou says. 'I stole many good years from you.'

'A life isn't measured in hours and minutes. It's the quality, not the length. All things considered, I've been luckier than most. Almost sixteen good years on Earth, and I've already had eight good ones here. I expect to have almost eight more before all's said and done. Nearly thirty-two years total, and that's not too shabby.'

'You're seven years old now? You seem very mature.'

'Well, I'm seven–eight now, and it's different than being plain seven. I would have been twenty-four, you know,' Liz says. 'I do feel myself getting younger some days.'

'What does it feel like?' Amadou asks.

Liz thinks for a moment before she answers. 'Like falling asleep one minute, like waking up the next. Sometimes I forget. Sometimes I'm worried I will forget.' Liz laughs. 'I remember the first day I felt truly young. It was when my little brother, Alvy, turned twelve. I had turned eleven that same year.'

'It must be strange,' Amadou says. 'This getting younger.'

Liz shrugs. 'You get older, you get younger, and I'm not sure the difference is as great as I once thought. Would you like a balloon for your son?'

'Thank you,' Amadou replies, selecting a red one from a large bouqet of balloons that sits by Liz's desk. 'How did you know my son was here?' he asks.

'I've been watching you off and on for years,' Liz admits. 'I know he is a good boy and I know you are a good man.'

Childhood

Owen is six, and Liz is four.

When the weather is fine, they spend afternoons in Betty's garden. He wears a paper crown, she a pink tutu.

On the last of a fortnight of fine days, Liz places an old copy of *Tuck Everlasting* in Owen's lap.

'What's that for?' Owen asks.

'Story?' Liz smiles sweetly, revealing brand-new baby teeth.

'I don't want to read your stupid girl book,' Owen says. 'Read it yourself.'

Liz decides to take Owen's advice. She picks up the book and holds it in front of her. And then, the strangest thing happens. She finds she cannot read. Maybe it's my eyes, she thinks. She squints at the text, but it makes no difference.

'Owen,' says Liz, 'there's something wrong with this book.'

'Let me see it,' Owen says. He opens the book, inspects it,

and returns it to her. 'There's nothing wrong with it, Liz,' he declares.

Liz holds the book as close to her eyes as she can and then at arm's length. Although she does not know why, she laughs. She hands it to Owen. 'You do it,' she commands.

'Oh, all right,' Owen says. 'Honestly, Liz, you're such a bore.' He removes the bookmark and begins to read from *Tuck Everlasting* with a distinct lack of feeling: ' *"Pa thinks it's something left over from—well, from some other plan for the way the world should be," ' said Jesse. "Some plan that didn't work out too good. And so everything was changed. Except that the spring was passed over, somehow or other. Maybe he's right. I don't know. But you see—" '*

Liz interrupts him. 'Owen.'

Owen tosses the book aside, frustrated. 'What is it now? You shouldn't ask a person to read just to interrupt.'

'Owen,' Liz continues, 'do you remember that game?'

'What game?'

'We were big,' says Liz, 'I was soooo big, bigger every day, and our faces were like this all the time.' Liz frowns and furrows her brow in an exaggerated fashion. 'And there was a house and a school. And a car and a job and a dog! And I was old! I was more old than you! And everything was rush-rush quick, and hard, so hard.' Liz laughs again, a chortling little bird call of a laugh.

After a moment, Owen answers, 'I remember.'

'I wonder,' says Liz, 'I wonder what was so . . . hard?'

'It was just a dumb game, Liz.'

'It was a dumb game,' Liz agrees. 'Let's not play it anymore.'

Owen nods. 'We won't.'

'I think I was . . . I think I was . . . I was dead.' Liz begins to cry.

Owen can't stand to see Liz cry. He takes Liz in his arms. She is so small now. When had that happened? he wonders. 'Don't be scared, Liz,' he says, 'it was just a game, remember.'

'Oh, right,' she says, 'I forgot.'

'May I continue your story now?' Owen asks, picking up the book.

Liz nods, and Owen begins to read again.

' "But you see, Winnie Foster, when I told you before I'm a hundred and four years old, I was telling the truth. But I'm really only seventeen. And, so far as I know, I'll stay seventeen till the end of the world." ' Owen sets down the book. 'That's the end of the chapter. Should I read the next one?'

'Please,' says Liz, sticking her thumb happily into her mouth.

Owen sighs and continues to read. 'Winnie did not believe in fairy tales. She had never longed for a magic wand, did not expect to marry a prince, and was scornful—most of the time— of her grandmother's elves. So now she sat, mouth open, wide-eyed, not knowing what to make of this extraordinary story. It couldn't—not a bit of it—be true . . .'

Liz closes her eyes, and it isn't very long before she falls into a sweet, untroubled sleep.

Birth

On a mild January morning just before dawn, Betty delivers
Liz to the launch nurse.

'You look familiar,' Dolly says, gently taking the baby from
Betty. 'Do I know you from somewhere?'

Betty shakes her head.

'The baby, she looks familiar, too.' The nurse holds Liz up to
get a better view. 'She looked just like you, I bet.'

'Yes,' Betty says, 'yes.'

Dolly tickles Liz under the chin. 'Pretty baby,' she coos. The
nurse lays Liz on the table and begins swaddling her.

'Please.' Betty places her hand on the nurse's. 'Not too tight.'

'Don't worry,' Dolly says pleasantly. 'I've done this before.'

Many more people attend Liz's second Release than had her
first.

In addition to Betty, there is Aldous Ghent who looks much the same as when Liz first met him. He has more hair now.

And Shelly carries Thandi in a bassinet. Thandi will be making her own journey very soon. She, of course, has less hair now.

And Curtis wears a dark suit, although the custom is to wear white at births.

And, of course, Owen is there, too. He is accompanied by Emily Reilly (formerly Welles), who now acts as his occasional babysitter. She tries to interest Owen in the proceedings, but he prefers to play with his toy boat in a puddle. 'Don't run off, O,' Emily tells him before joining the others to watch the Release.

Owen doesn't watch when they place Liz in the River, next to all the other babies who would be born that day. Nor does he watch when the launch nurse pushes Liz away from the shore into the current that leads back to Earth. To the untrained observer, it seems as if Liz's departure has no effect on Owen whatsoever.

Curtis Jest watches Owen before deciding to go over to him.

'Owen,' Curtis asks, 'do you remember who that was?'

Owen looks up from playing with the boat. He appears to find Curtis's question very difficult. 'Lizzie?'

'Yes,' says Curtis, 'that was Lizzie. She was my friend. She was your . . . your friend, too.'

Owen continues playing with the boat. He begins singing Liz's name in the unaffected way children will sometimes sing a name. 'Lizzie, Lizzie, Lizzie,' he sings. Owen stops singing abruptly and looks up at Curtis. A horrified expression crosses

Owen's face. 'Is she . . . gone?'

'Yes,' says Curtis.

Owen nods. 'Gonegonegonegonegone.' Owen begins to cry in an undignified manner, although he isn't entirely sure why he is crying. Curtis takes Owen's hand, leading Owen away from the puddle.

'You know,' says Curtis, 'you may see her again someday.'

'Cool,' says Owen, and with that, he stops crying.

From across the parking lot, Betty claps her hands. 'Cigars and champagne back at the house!'

At Curtis and Betty's house, a pink and white 'It's a girl!' banner hangs on the door. Curtis passes out cigars with pink ribbons tied around them. A "Happy Birthday, Liz" sheet cake is served in addition to champagne and punch.

Aldous Ghent eats a forkful of cake and begins to cry. 'Birthday cake always depresses me,' he says to no one in particular.

Everyone stops talking when Betty clinks a spoon against a champagne flute. 'If you wouldn't mind indulging me, I'd like to say a few words about Liz,' she says. 'Liz was my granddaughter, of course. But if she hadn't come to Elsewhere, I never would have known her at all. I died before she was born.

'Liz was my granddaughter, but also a good friend. She was just a girl when she got here, but she grew into a fine woman. She liked to laugh and she loved spending time with her dogs and her friends. I never would have met my husband if Liz hadn't come into my life.' Betty takes Curtis by the hand.

'On Elsewhere, we fool ourselves into thinking we know what will be just because we know the amount of time we have left.

266

We know this, but we never really know what will be.

'We never know what will happen,' Betty says, 'but I believe good things happen every day. I believe good things happen even when bad things happen. And I believe on a happy day like today, we can still feel a little sad. And that's life, isn't it?' Betty raises her glass. 'To Liz!'

What Liz Thinks

It was a pleasant enough life, Liz thinks. Though she could not remember the specific events, she senses something wonderful happened once. And she feels good about the prospects for the next.

Looking at the babies to her rear and fore, left and right, she notices that most of them keep their eyes closed. Why do they keep their eyes closed? she wonders. Don't they know there's so much to see?

As Liz travels down the River, farther and farther away from her home, farther and farther away from Elsewhere, she has many thoughts. Indeed, there is much time for rumination when one is a baby at the start of a long journey.

There is no difference in quality between a life lived forward and a life lived backward, she thinks. She had come to love this backward life. It was, after all, the only life she had.

Furthermore, she isn't sad to be a baby. As the wisest here know, it isn't a sad thing getting older. On Earth, the attempt to stay young, in the face of maturity, is futile. And it isn't a sad thing growing younger, either. There was a time Liz was afraid that she would forget things, but by the time she truly began to forget, she forgot to be afraid to forget. Life is kind, the baby thinks.

The waves cradle the babies and rock them to sleep. And before long, this one succumbs, too.

She sleeps; she sleeps.

And when she sleeps, she dreams.

And when she dreams, she dreams of a girl who was lost at sea but one day found the shore.

Epilogue: At the Beginning

The baby, a girl, is born at 6:24 a.m.

She weighs six pounds, ten ounces.

The mother takes the baby in her arms and asks her, 'Who are you, my little one?'

And in response, this baby, who is Liz and not Liz at the same time, laughs.

Acknowledgments

An exceptionally comely, kind, lovely, and large group of people are responsible for the tome you find in your hands. I wish to thank my editor at FSG, Janine O'Malley, who is always right, completely indefatigable, and the most fun. I wish to thank my agents: Jonathan Pecarsky, who is unfailingly hopeful and truthful, and Andy McNicol, who fights the good fight. I wish to thank my editor at Bloomsbury UK, Sarah Odedina, whose enthusiasm and conviction was Elsewhere's sun. I wish to thank Richard and AeRan Zevin—it is my great fortune to have parents who are also excellent readers. I wish to thank my pug, Mrs. DeWinter (D-Dub), who tries to teach me the language of dogs every day—I have proven a slow pupil indeed. I wish to thank my partner of the last ten years, Hans Canosa, who read every draft of the book and always believed.

I also wish to thank Kerry Barden, Anna DeRoy, Tracy Fisher, Eugenie Furniss, Stuart Gelwarg, Nancy Goldenberg, Shana Kelly, Mary Lawless, Brian Steinberg, and everyone at William Morris, Bloomsbury, and especially at Farrar, Straus and Giroux.